The Cowboy and the Doctor

The Cowboy and the Doctor

A Gallaghers of Montana Romance

Eve Gaddy

TULE
PUBLISHING

Chapter One

H E WAS THE last Gallagher bachelor.

Half an hour before, Wyatt and Mia had tied the knot, putting an end to Wyatt's single status and leaving Dylan the lone bachelor among the men of his family.

Maybe there was something in the water. If so, he'd be very careful about what he drank. He liked his sisters-in-law, including the brand-new one, Mia. Jack, Sean and Wyatt all seemed happy. They wanted to be married, wanted to settle down with one woman. That was great. For them.

So far, he'd take his horses over any woman. He liked women. He liked them a lot. Liked being around them, liked talking to them, really liked having sex with them. But one woman? Forever?

Not him. He hadn't met a woman yet who tempted him to give up his freedom.

Not that there weren't some women he found pretty damn intriguing. Dr. Samantha Striker being the most recent.

Though she'd worked at Marietta Regional Hospital for

close to a year now, Dylan had only met her a couple of weeks before. His new stallion kicked Clay Landers, one of his longtime ranch hands and Dylan's right-hand man, in the abdomen and it was serious enough that Dylan took him to the hospital instead of waiting for an ambulance.

Dr. Striker, the trauma surgeon, had taken Clay to have emergency surgery quickly, but the process took a lot longer than Dylan had hoped it would. He waited around until she came to talk to him afterwards. Wearing baby-blue scrubs, a scrub cap, and with a surgical mask hanging from her neck, she looked pretty solemn, but when she saw him she put on a reassuring smile that didn't particularly reassure him.

Dylan was no doctor, but with three brothers who were, he knew a little about medicine. Especially farm accidents.

"I'm Samantha Striker, the trauma surgeon," she said, offering a hand. "We didn't actually meet when you brought in Mr. Landers."

"Dylan Gallagher," he said, shaking hands. "No, you got him up to the OR in record time."

"Internal bleeding isn't something to fool around with. You did the right thing bringing him in. I suspect it would have taken an ambulance quite a while to get out to your ranch."

"Good. I worried about that, but his injury seemed serious and I was afraid to wait. How is he, Doc?"

"Before surgery, he said I could talk to the boss about the accident and his surgery. I take it you're the boss?"

"Yes." And it was Dylan's hellion horse who'd kicked the crap out of Clay. "Is he going to be okay?"

She hesitated almost imperceptibly before answering. "He should be, but it's a serious injury. He had a liver laceration, which caused internal bleeding. We repaired it, but he'll need to stay in the hospital for some time. I can't say how long at this point."

"I'm not sure how long he'll stay in the hospital. He hates them. No offense."

"None taken."

He looked at her a minute before asking, "Is there something you're not telling me, Doc?"

"Why do you ask?"

"I have three brothers who are doctors. I can tell when they're bullshitting me."

She smiled at that. "I knew who you were the minute I saw you. You and your brothers bear a strong resemblance to each other. And no, I'm not bullshitting you. He should recover from the accident."

"Those are carefully chosen words. If I were on his HIPAA, could you tell me what it is you're worried about?"

"Are you on his HIPAA?"

"No. So I'll just wait until you talk to Clay and he'll tell me."

She pulled off her cap and rubbed the back of her neck. Thick, wavy, blonde hair reached her shoulders. Damn, a very pretty blonde. Dylan really went for blondes. And redheads and brunettes. But especially blondes.

"I'll give you a call when he wakes up."

"Thanks. Say, Doc, what are you doing tomorrow night?"

She blinked at him. "Are you asking me out?"

"Why, is that a problem?"

"Not exactly a problem. But I have a boyfriend."

"Damn. That's too bad. Let me know if you two break up, okay?"

She laughed. "You'll be the first to know."

SO THAT'S DYLAN GALLAGHER. God, he was cute. And nice. And a cowboy. Sam had a real weakness for cowboys.

Rumor had it he was a flirt. A man who'd never been serious about a woman, at least as far as anyone in Marietta knew. And that was enough to make Sam very wary. Her shift had just ended and she was supposed to meet her friend, Bianca, to go for a run. Most of the time they ran in the morning, but it depended on their work schedules. She went home and since it was cold outside, put on several layers of clothes, along with a knit hat and gloves. Bianca lived a few houses down and on the next street over, which made running together handy.

Bianca Whitehall was a family practice doctor who had recently become partners with Jack Gallagher in his family practice clinic. She was also the person who had convinced

Sam to move to Marietta when she decided to leave Dallas. Sam had wanted to go someplace completely different from the big city, and Marietta was definitely different. It still had a small-town atmosphere, though the hospital and medical community had grown enough in recent years to require more specialists. The hospital had become a level III trauma center, which entailed quite a few more personnel than Marietta had. Therefore a lot of the doctors were new.

"Tell me I'll feel better once we start," Sam said when Bianca met her. She needed something to help her unwind. During Clay Landers' emergency surgery she'd had an unwelcome surprise. Ultimately she'd diagnosed colon cancer and performed a colectomy of the tumor. While his cancer had been detected at an early stage, he wasn't in the clear yet and wouldn't be for some time to come.

Starting to stretch and warm up, Bianca asked, "What's wrong? Bad day?"

"Parts of it."

"Anything you want to talk about?"

"Not really." They started off slow, planning on a fairly short run since they both liked to do their long runs in the mornings.

After a bit, Bianca said, "So, Dylan Gallagher."

Sam eyed her warily. "What about him?"

"I saw you two talking earlier at the hospital. I didn't realize you knew Dylan."

"I didn't until today. I operated on one of his employees

earlier today."

"What did you think?"

"About what?"

"Not what, who."

"Oh, you mean Dylan? He seems like a nice guy."

"He is. Also hot."

Sam laughed. "Yes, he is. Very."

"Did he ask you out?"

Sam gave her a considering look. "Yes. How did you know?"

"Lucky guess. So when are you going out?"

"We're not." She shrugged. "You know I don't date players."

"You haven't dated anyone, period, in months."

Instead of answering, Sam said, "I've got a stitch in my side. I need to walk."

Bianca slowed down but, naturally, didn't let the subject drop. "Dylan's not a player. Not really."

"How can you *not really* be a player? You either are or you aren't."

"In that case, he's not. He doesn't screw around on the woman he's with. Players do."

Sam snorted but didn't say anything.

"Tell me you didn't claim the imaginary boyfriend."

"Why not? It's the most effective way to turn down a guy."

"But why turn him down?"

Bianca knew very well why Sam wasn't into dating but she wouldn't stop trying to change her mind. "I'm not interested. If you're so hot to trot about him, you date him."

"I already have. We dated for a while when I first came to town."

Sam shot her a skeptical glance. "What happened?"

"Nothing major. We decided it wasn't working."

"And you still like him?"

"Everyone does," she said simply. "I don't know of one of his ex-girlfriends who dislikes him. He's a great guy. You should give him a chance."

"I'll think about it," Sam said. But they both knew she wouldn't.

Chapter Two

"HOW ARE YOU doing, Clay?" Dylan asked his friend the following day. "I saw you yesterday after the surgery but you might not remember. You were pretty out of it."

"Feel like shit," Clay said. "How's Trouble?"

"He's fine. You're the one who's injured." Dylan sat in the only chair in the room.

"He'll come around."

"I hope so." But he sure as hell wouldn't guarantee it.

"Did the doc tell you what she found?"

"Besides your hard head? No. I'm not on your HIPAA so she can't tell me anything unless you give her the okay."

"Yeah, this hippa, happa, hoppa or whatever it is. Okay if I put you on it?"

"Of course." Clay didn't have anyone else. The Gallaghers were his family. "What did she find?"

"Dr. Striker says I have cancer. Colon cancer."

"Oh, shit. I knew something else was going on but damn, that sucks."

"Yep. It surely does."

Dylan asked him for more details but Clay was slim on them. Either because he was tired by then or because he didn't know. Or maybe he just didn't want to think about it. Which Dylan could understand.

"Try not to worry." Stupid, but what else could he say? "We'll make sure you're taken care of. Jack's your regular doctor, isn't he?"

"I guess. He's been by. He's bent out of shape about it all. But hell, I haven't been to see him since you made me get that tetanus shot a few years back. I don't know why he'd think anything was his fault."

Dylan remembered he'd had the devil of a time getting Clay to any doctor at all. He only managed it by threatening to fire him if he didn't go. Tetanus wasn't something to fool around with.

Jack, the eldest Gallagher brother, had come back to Marietta after his training and been there ever since. He and his wife, Maya, had a blended family. Each had a daughter from a previous marriage and they had a baby son together.

Dylan knew his brother well enough to know that he would feel responsible for Clay, even though none of this was Jack's fault. It's hard to diagnose a disease when the person won't come in to see you.

"You look tired." How old was Clay, anyway? Not much older than Jack, Dylan thought. The surgery had taken its toll. Lying in a hospital bed with tubes everywhere, he looked nothing like the man who never tired and worked harder than anyone except Dylan himself. "I'll come back tomorrow and we can talk about what the doctor thinks you should do."

"She says I need chemo." He gave a disgusted grunt. "Can you see me at the hospital every week? For who knows how many weeks?" He tried to sit up but instead fell back. "It's a bunch of crap," he finished weakly.

Dylan didn't argue. He wanted to talk to the doctor to find out what exactly he would have to convince Clay to do. No sense fighting that fight before he had to.

"Get some rest. I'll see you tomorrow."

Before heading back to the ranch Dylan stopped by the Java Café. The coffee shop on Main Street was one of his favorite places to go when he came into town. He liked their white chocolate mocha latte. While Glory, the Gallaghers' longtime cook and housekeeper, made great coffee and even better food, she did not make lattes. If Dylan wanted a latte he had to go to town to get it.

"Thanks, Sally," he said to the barista when she handed him his coffee.

"No trouble at all, Dylan." She added with a flirty smile, "I added extra whipped cream, just the way you like it."

He smiled and thanked her again. He admitted he was worried about Clay. He didn't know whether talking to the doctor would ease his mind or make him more worried. He took a seat at one of the tables and tried to decide if he should call Dr. Striker or try to catch her when she did rounds. Evening rounds, maybe. His mornings were pretty much taken up with ranch chores. Idly, he looked out the window and saw the back of a blonde wearing scrubs walking into the café.

Samantha Striker walked in. She gave Sally her order and went to the other end of the counter to wait for her drink.

Dylan got up and walked over to her. "Hi, Doc."

She turned around and smiled. "Hi, Dylan. Clay was asking for you this morning. Have you seen him?"

"Yes, I just came from the hospital. In fact, you're just the person I wanted to see. Can you sit with me a minute?"

"Of course." She picked up her drink and followed him to the small table he'd chosen by the window in the corner. The coffee shop was a popular place in Marietta and also a place where gossip circulated. The tables were grouped close together, and for a moment, Dylan worried that someone might overhear them discussing Clay's case. Luckily, the shop wasn't too busy at the moment and the nearby tables were empty.

He got right to the point. "Clay put me on his HIPAA."

"Good. He told me he intended to." She sipped her coffee and said, "What do you want to know?"

"Whatever you can tell me. Clay said you found cancer when you operated on him. But he wasn't at all clear about what that meant, or even what you'd done. I wasn't sure if that was because he didn't know much or if the pain meds were making him loopy."

"A little of both, probably. He might not have completely taken in what I told him. Most people hear the word cancer and that's the last thing they hear. I'm glad he told you, though. I asked him if a family member could be with him and he told me to talk to you. I didn't realize you were family."

"Maybe not technically, but Clay's been working for us and living on the ranch since he was a teenager. I'm not sure what happened to his parents but he said he grew up in foster care and took off on his own as soon as he could. So, yeah, I guess I'm as much family as anyone."

While Clay wasn't the ranch foreman, he was second only to Dylan in the horse-breeding operation. In fact, he was damn near irreplaceable, besides being a longtime friend.

Cancer, damn it. Dylan couldn't help thinking of his mother, who had died from cancer when he was very young. "How bad is it, Doc?"

DYLAN LOOKED WORRIED. Sam wished he didn't have reason to be. "During surgery I found some suspicious signs and ultimately found a tumor in his colon. I resected a small section of his colon. He'll most likely need chemotherapy and potentially more surgery, but unless he goes elsewhere to an oncologist, that will be up to his primary care physician and what they find when they run tests."

"What's his prognosis?"

"I can give you percentages, but that's not all there is to it. Attitude matters too."

"So it's not good."

"I didn't say that."

"Come on, Doc. Don't bullshit me."

Sam sighed. Dylan was obviously a person who needed all the facts, the bad as well as the good. It didn't really surprise her that he wanted her to give it to him straight. As he'd said the first time they met, he had three brothers who were doctors. "Clay has stage II colon cancer. The five-year survival rate is eighty-seven percent."

"So it's good unless you're one of the thirteen percent."

True, even if it wasn't the most hopeful outlook. "Yes. However, it's fortunate we caught it when we did. If not for the accident it might have progressed much further before it was diagnosed."

"Oh, great," Dylan said with disgust. "So the fact that my horse kicked the crap out of him and damn near killed him is a good thing."

"It might be. The fact that he had to come to the hospital was good. From what he's said, he doesn't go to the doctor unless it's unavoidable."

"Yeah, that's an understatement. Jack tries but Clay's pretty damn stubborn." He rubbed his hand over his face. "How much help is he going to need?"

"That depends on a lot of factors. It would be beneficial

if you or someone else he trusts can go with him to his first post-op appointment as well as his first appointment with your brother. Jack is his primary care physician, isn't he?"

"Technically. I think the last time he saw Jack was five or six years ago. As for going with him, that's going to be tough. Clay's not going to go for that. I can hear him now telling me he doesn't need a babysitter and he can damn well take care of himself."

"It's very important for him to have a support system. He'll also need help getting to and from his chemo appointments."

"Understood."

"Will he be able to depend on his job?"

"His job?" Dylan asked, puzzled. "You mean keeping his job?"

"Yes." Not everyone was able to keep a person on while he went through chemo and any other treatments the cancer might require.

"Of course he'll keep his job. I told you, he's family."

"He could be out for quite some time," she warned him.

"So I'll hire temporary help. Until Clay gets back on his feet."

"I'm glad. The less stress he has to handle the better. Knowing he can count on his job, and you, will help."

"I can't guarantee he'll have no stress but we'll take care of him. I'm the one who's going to have the problem. Clay is my right-hand man. He helps me run the breeding operation. He's really great with the horses."

"I thought a horse kicked him?"

"That's right. But it can happen to anyone. Besides, this was my problem child who kicked him."

"Your problem child?"

"My new stallion. He's got some issues."

Just then a woman walked by, bumped into Dylan and dropped her cup beside him. He caught the cup before it hit the ground and handed it to the woman.

"Oh, Dylan, I'm so sorry. I'm the clumsiest thing," she said. "Thank goodness it's a cold drink and not hot coffee."

"No harm done. How have you been, Kayla?"

The woman, a very pretty busty brunette, tossed long, dark hair over her shoulder. "I'm doing fine. I haven't seen you at Grey's lately."

"No, I haven't been in much. Kayla Harrison, meet Dr. Samantha Striker," he said, motioning between the two.

"Nice to meet you," Sam said.

"You too," Kayla said unenthusiastically, barely glancing at Sam. In fact, she looked a little peeved.

Sam hid a smile, wondering if the woman thought she and Dylan were more than acquaintances and that explained her air of annoyance.

Kayla's expression changed to alarm. "Wait a minute. *Doctor* Striker? You're not sick, are you Dylan?" She put her hand on his shoulder.

"Not a bit," Dylan said cheerfully.

"Oh, well that's good." She glanced at Sam, as if expecting her to leave.

Sam simply smiled and stayed put.

"Good to see you, Kayla."

"You too, Dylan." With a last, reluctant glance at Dylan, she left.

"Should I have excused myself?" Sam asked curiously.

"What? No, why would you?"

"I gathered your friend would have appreciated some time alone with you."

"Kayla? I don't know why she would."

Sam tilted her head and studied him for a moment. Was he really that oblivious? "Because she likes you?"

He looked surprised. "I don't think so. Not that way, anyway."

The hell she didn't. And who could blame her? Not me. Dylan Gallagher was very appealing and apparently, a nice guy. Not that she was looking for a man, nice or otherwise. Regardless of what her friend Bianca thought, Sam's biological clock wasn't ticking. She liked men a lot. Unfortunately, her past entanglements had not worked out well.

"Getting back to Clay," Dylan said, "we'll take care of him."

"Good. The better his support network, the better his outcome is likely to be."

"So they say," he said skeptically. "Sometimes it doesn't matter."

"You sound like you're speaking from personal experience."

He hesitated, then shrugged. "My mother died when I was six. Lung cancer. She never smoked a day in her life. And she had a decent support system, at least according to my brothers, she did. I was too little to understand much of what went on, but I understood when she died."

Sam put a hand on his arm. "I'm so sorry, Dylan."

He shrugged again. "Don't bother telling me things are different now and that there have been huge advances in cancer care. I've heard it all. From my brothers."

"They're right. But it's like you said earlier, the odds don't matter if you're one of the unlucky ones." She patted his arm. "All I can tell you is it will help Clay more if you can be positive. At least around Clay. And it might help you too."

He didn't say anything but she could see he was still brooding. It was hard to walk the line between reassuring someone and being too optimistic in a situation that could turn out badly. "Would you feel better if we sent him to an oncologist for a second opinion? I know of a good one in Billings."

He gave her a wry grin. "No, I trust you and Jack. More importantly, Clay trusts Jack, at least as much as he trusts any doctor. Besides, we're going to have enough trouble getting Clay to his treatments here, much less in Billings or Bozeman."

Chapter Three

A FEW DAYS after talking to Samantha Striker at the Java Café, Dylan led his new stallion out to the round pen. He should have known not to buy a horse named Trouble. But one look at him and Dylan had fallen for him.

He was a beauty. A beautiful buckskin Norwegian Fjord. Creamy tan coat, black stockings and nose, with the distinctive bi-color black and white mane of the Norwegian Fjord. Officially the color was called brunblakk. Or brown dun in English. Dylan had bought him planning to breed him but Trouble was, well, trouble.

Trouble didn't care for people. Poor Clay was proof of that.

The damn horse had bitten people, kicked people, and in general was difficult as hell. Dylan had even asked Sean, his horse-whisperer brother, to help him out but Trouble was one horse who didn't respond to Sean's magic way with horses. Dylan was aware Trouble had been abused, though his previous owner insisted the horse came to him squirrelly and afraid of people and that he'd had no hand in abusing the animal. At any rate, Trouble had come to the Gallagher ranch with a bad attitude and scars to match. Sean recommended he keep trying, and thought the horse would come around given time.

Trouble hadn't exactly come around, but he and Dylan had come to an uneasy truce. Uneasy because Dylan didn't trust him not to kick the shit out of him if given half a chance. Dylan was still working on breaking him and, frankly, he didn't have time to spend coddling one animal. But neither did he want to let him go. Something about Trouble got to him and Dylan had always been a sucker for an animal in need. Whether he knew it or not, Trouble needed people.

Dylan would just have to be patient and hope he found the key to Trouble's heart. He cooled down Trouble, groomed him and put him up. Then headed for the hospital to see his friend.

When he got there, Clay was in a piss-poor mood. Clay didn't want to talk about his cancer. Not to Dylan and, he suspected, not to anyone. Dylan knew he'd seen Jack by now, but he wasn't sure his brother had been able to get through to him. Clay put them off, saying he'd do something about the cancer after he got out of the hospital. One problem at a time, he'd told them.

Whenever Dylan visited, the first thing Clay asked for was an update on Trouble. There wasn't a lot to say other than *he's the same ornery stallion he's been since I got him.*

Still, there was one good thing about Clay being at the hospital. It gave Dylan a chance to see Samantha when he visited his friend.

Clay gave him shit about it every time Dylan came to see him. He knew damn well his boss was there to see Sam every bit as much as him. Dylan saw no point in arguing since Clay was spot on in his analysis.

He would have kept a close eye on Clay anyway, but the chance of seeing Samantha made the trip into town even more worthwhile.

SAM HAD PUT in a long day in surgery and since she had that night and the next day off she had big plans. They revolved around sleep, ordering pizza to be delivered and not getting out of her jammies until she had to go to work on Sunday.

On her way out of the hospital she ran into Bianca. They talked for a minute and as they parted Bianca said, "I'll see you at seven."

Mystified, Sam looked at her.

"You forgot," her friend said accusingly.

She started to deny it but quickly decided there was no point to that. "What did I forget?"

"My party. Tonight at Grey's Saloon."

"Your—" *Shit.* She broke off as she remembered. "Of course I didn't forget your birthday. What kind of friend does that?" *Me,* she thought guiltily. Going to Bianca's birthday bash had *so* not been in her plans.

Her friend, who knew perfectly well that Sam had completely forgotten, merely raised an eyebrow. "I can count on you then?"

"I wouldn't miss it." Crap. If she hurried she might get a nap in before she went. Then she remembered she didn't have a present for Bianca so that blew that idea out of the water as well.

Sam headed to Marietta Western Wear. Even though she had grown up in Montana, as far as Sam knew, her friend had never even been on a horse. But she liked to dress western. It didn't take long to pick out a satin western-style shirt with lots of bling. Exactly the kind of thing Bianca would love. She hoped, anyway.

She was waiting for the clerk to wrap it when Dylan Gallagher walked in. This was at least the fifth time she'd seen him in as many days. Several times at the hospital when he was visiting Clay, once at Java Café, and today.

Dylan wore a cowboy hat, scuffed boots, blue jeans and a thick shearling coat. He looked like exactly what he was. A hardworking cowboy. Damn, the man was hot. He was bound to know it too. But he didn't seem conceited or full of himself, she thought, remembering his demeanor at the coffee shop. No, not conceited at all. She knew why people liked him. So far, she couldn't tell that there was anything *not* to like about him.

That annoyed the shit out of her.

He took off his hat and smiled at her. His hair was a dark brown, almost black, wavy and reaching to his collar. He hadn't shaved but on him it looked good. *I'm not falling for that good old boy charm. Been there, done that, and I'm not doing it again.*

But there was more to him than just the charm. He cared. About his friends, his family, his horses.

There was bound to be something wrong with him. Otherwise he'd be married by now. She knew he was the youngest Gallagher, but she didn't know exactly how old he was. Had to be late twenties or early thirties.

"Hi, Doc. How are you?"

"Hi, Dylan. I'm good." His eyes were green. A kind of dreamy moss green, rather than emerald or jade. She wondered if they changed color with his mood. "Tell me something, Dylan."

"Ask away."

"How did we go more than six months without ever meeting but since I operated on Clay we've seen each other almost daily?"

He grinned, slow and sexy. "Just lucky, I guess."

She narrowed her eyes at him. "Did you plan this?"

"Plan what?"

"Running into me here. Running into me all the time." Jeesh. She sounded paranoid.

Dylan laughed outright. "No, but it's an idea. Still got that boyfriend?"

She had an urge to tell him the truth. Instead she said,

"Same answer as the first time you asked me."

"Too bad. I'm still hoping."

The clerk came back and gave Sam her package. "Dylan, hi. We haven't seen you around in a while."

The girl all but batted her eyes at him. It didn't appear to affect him. He smiled and said, "Yep, the ranch has been keeping me busy."

She placed her hand on his arm and gave it a little pat. "Lily's having a party tomorrow night. You should come."

"I'll do my best," Dylan said.

"Do that." She smiled and left to help another customer.

"You don't have any intention of going, do you?" Sam asked him.

"Probably not." He considered her a moment. "Why? Did you want to go with me?"

"Boyfriend, remember?"

"Oh, yeah. Forgot about him."

She knew damn well he hadn't forgotten since she'd told him five minutes before but she didn't call him on it. She had a feeling he knew, or at least suspected, that her boyfriend was purely fictional.

"Good to see you, Doc." He held open the door for her and she went out, conscious of the temptation to find out if he was any different from the men in her past.

Maybe he was, though she doubted it. She had better sense than to fall for a charming, good-looking and very hot cowboy. Didn't she?

Chapter Four

DYLAN PROBABLY WOULDN'T have gone to Bianca Whitehall's birthday bash, but he had a good reason to be at the party tonight. And the reason was sitting over at the bar in Grey's Saloon looking like a million bucks in a short skirt, cowboy boots and with her pretty blonde hair flowing free past her shoulders.

Samantha Striker fascinated him. More every time he saw her. At first he'd put it down to the fact that she kept turning him down. He was almost a hundred percent certain that her boyfriend was a figment of her imagination. But he'd been rejected before and normally he shrugged and went on about his business. He couldn't do that with Samantha.

The fact that he'd seen her almost daily for the past two weeks had pretty well made it impossible to forget about her. Not to mention she was Clay's doctor. She'd given it to him straight the other day at Java Café. He appreciated that. But she'd also been compassionate both about Clay's case and to him when he'd talked about his mother's death.

Compassion was a common character trait among doctors. His brothers were doctors and they all had it. But there was something special about Samantha, even if he couldn't quite pinpoint what that was.

It still surprised him that he'd mentioned his mother's death to Samantha. He didn't talk about it to a lot of people. Just his family and then only once in a while. And though he'd missed out on a lot growing up without a mother, his sister Glenna had done her best to mother him, even though she was only a little more than a year older than he was.

Glenna, who had disappeared from Argentina without a trace when she was accused of embezzlement. Damn, he was not going to think about Glenna tonight. The private detective was still looking for her and beyond that there was nothing he could do to find her.

He shook off that depressing thought and walked over to the bar. "Hi, Doc."

"Dylan? What—oh, that's right. You and Bianca are old friends."

"Do you need a refill?" he asked, gesturing at her beer.

"No, if I have more than one I'll fall asleep and Bianca probably won't talk to me for a week."

"Long day?"

She sipped her beer and said, "Very."

"Your boyfriend here tonight?" He glanced around as if he was looking for the guy.

"No. He lives in Dallas."

"Dallas? So you're doing the long-distance thing. Must be hard."

She shrugged. "Jeff's a doctor too. We're both heavily involved in our careers."

"Jeff. He has a name."

"Of course he has a name." She scowled at him. "It's Jeff. Jeff Lansing."

"He must not get out here much. No one here seems to have met him."

Her eyes narrowed and she frowned at him again. "Have you been asking around about me?"

"Settle down, Doc. I didn't have to ask. It's common knowledge."

"I wish you wouldn't call me Doc. My name is Samantha. Or Sam."

"Sorry. Your guy is quite the mystery, Samantha. Lots of speculation about him."

"That's one of the things about small towns that annoys the snot out of me," she said. "Everybody minds everyone else's business."

Dylan laughed. "You'll get used to it. They don't mean anything by it."

"Ha. I've been here for months and I'm not used to it yet."

Bianca came by just then. Dylan greeted her with a hug. "Happy birthday, Bianca."

"Thanks. Dylan. I'm so glad you could come tonight."

They chatted a bit about the weather, the hospital and riding horses. "Isn't that right, Sam?" Bianca said, including her in the conversation.

"Sorry, I wasn't paying attention. Isn't what right?"

"You were telling me just the other day how much you missed riding." Turning to Dylan, she said brightly, "Maybe she could ride one of your horses."

Sam shot her friend a dirty look, which Bianca ignored. "Olivia Canaday has a stables. I can ride there," Sam said.

"Oh, but you need to see Dylan's horses. He raises Norwegian Fjords. They're beautiful horses."

"I'm sure they are, but—"

"She's worried the boyfriend won't like it," Dylan told Bianca.

"Boyfriend? Oh, him. I'm sure Carson won't mind. Will he, Sam?"

Sam looked like she wanted to punch Bianca. "His name is Jeff. Which you know perfectly well."

"Damn. I never can remember his name." She winked at Dylan and left.

Score another point for the boyfriend being bogus. Dylan did his best not to smile. "It's no problem, Doc. I mean, Samantha. Bring him next time he's in town and you can both ride."

"Jeff doesn't ride."

"No? Well, that's no reason for you to miss out on something you enjoy. Have you been riding long?"

EVE GADDY

She nodded. "Since I was four or five. I grew up on a ranch in Texas."

Dylan tilted his head, considering her. "You're a cowgirl."

"Not anymore. Now I'm a doctor."

"Do you miss it?"

She took a sip of beer. "Sometimes. There are things I miss. My parents still live there. They've got a ranch in Aledo, a town outside of Fort Worth. I haven't been back since I moved up here. My parents have come up to see me, but it's hard for them to get away."

"What do you miss the most about the ranch?"

"Horses."

"I can remedy that."

"Uh-huh. I bet you can."

"You're awfully suspicious. What's wrong with a friendly ride?"

"Nothing. As long as that's all it is."

"Cross my heart," he said, suiting action to words. "I won't hit on you."

She didn't look like she believed him. "I'll think about it."

"I'll be waiting."

"Don't hold your breath. I only said I'd think about it."

"Got it." But it was a start. And the fact that the boyfriend was surely fictional didn't hurt, either.

SAM KNEW SHE shouldn't have but when Dylan asked her to dance she said yes. Somehow, one dance stretched into two, then three. By the time a slow song came on she didn't argue. Instead, she let him pull her into his arms and move to the music.

He held her firmly, but not too close. His hands stayed at her waist and didn't wander. He wore some kind of woodsy aftershave that smelled great. As they danced she drifted closer to him, enjoying the sensation of being held against a hard, masculine chest. She'd forgotten how to dance with someone who actually knew how to dance and didn't just shove her around the dance floor and expect her to fend for herself. She liked it. Too much.

"I shouldn't be dancing with you so much," she said, late in the evening, having lost count of the number of dances.

"Why?" he asked, smiling down at her.

"You know why."

"Because of your imaginary boyfriend?"

"No," she said, not bothering to dispute his words. "Because I like it too much."

He laughed and pulled her closer. "So do I, Sam."

Later on, Sam was standing in front of the mirror in the rest room putting on lip-gloss when Bianca appeared behind her.

"Well, well," Bianca said. "If it isn't Ms. I'm-not-interested herself."

"Wipe that smug grin off your face," Sam said to her

friend. She capped her lip-gloss and turned around to face Bianca.

"Why? I knew you two were perfect for each other. Obviously, I was right."

"You're jumping to a pretty huge conclusion there. We've been dancing. Only dancing."

"Yes, you've been *only dancing* for the last hour. I've seen the way you two look at each other. Only dancing, my butt."

Sam saw no point in arguing. "Dylan knows I've been lying about having a boyfriend. I haven't admitted it yet, but he knows."

"No surprise there. It's obvious you don't. You don't act like you're committed to anyone."

"I suppose not."

"Well, don't be so glum about it. Dylan's a good guy. Can't you just have some fun?"

"I don't know. It's been a long time since I tried."

"And we both know why." She paused and added softly, "You've got a new life here, Sam. It's time you lived it instead of letting it pass you by."

"That's not what I'm doing," she protested, guiltily aware that there was more than a grain of truth to what Bianca had said.

"It's been more than a year. When are you going to forgive yourself for something that you weren't responsible for?"

"It isn't that simple."

"Yes, it is. You've punished yourself enough, Sam. You

deserve something good to happen to you."

"And you think that something good is Dylan Gallagher?"

"I think he could be. If you let him."

"I'll think about it," she told Bianca, just as she'd told Dylan.

Bianca was right. Sam knew that she had not been responsible for Gary Baxter's actions. Not for any of them, and particularly not for the final act that sent him to prison.

But that didn't make his wife Amber any less dead.

Chapter Five

DYLAN WALKED SAM to her car. She'd parked in the lot by the courthouse, so it didn't take long to get there. The night was cold and clear, the stars bright and plentiful. "I had fun tonight," she told him, mindful of her talk with Bianca.

"I did, too. Tell me something, Sam."

"Okay, what?"

"Why the lie? Your boyfriend is pure fiction, isn't he?"

She started to deny it but after looking at Dylan, she knew it would be pointless. Tired of maintaining the fiction, she told him the truth. "It's easier than explaining over and over again that I don't want to date."

"Why don't you want to date?" He leaned back against her car hood, hands in pockets.

Was Bianca right? Was Sam punishing herself and that's why she'd stopped dating? Or was it simpler than that?

"I choose the wrong men. I think they're good guys and then I wind up getting burned. My judgment concerning men, or at least, the men I go out with, is crap. I always fall for someone who's going to hurt me."

"So you stopped dating altogether? Don't you think that's a little drastic?"

"No. I think it's entirely reasonable." She rubbed her arms. "I'm freezing. If we're going to talk let's get in my car and let me turn on the heater."

"Suits me."

"My last three relationships were a complete bust," she said after they got settled inside the car.

"All for the same reason?"

She shrugged. "More or less. One was married, which I didn't know until after we got involved. I broke it off when I found out. The next man was very charming and completely incapable of being faithful. Which I also broke off after discovering he was cheating on me. The last one was a sweetheart. But he was a player. After that I more or less swore off men."

"Aha. Now I see why you don't like me. You think I'm a player."

"I do like you. That's the problem. I like you but...you have a certain reputation."

He stretched his arm across the back of her seat and toyed with her hair. "And what is this reputation?"

"You know exactly what it is. You're nice, you're charming, you're hot and you've never dated anyone seriously. At least as far as anyone here knows. Are you going to deny it?"

He laughed. "I can't really answer about the first part,

but it's true I've never been serious about a woman. I have nothing against it, though. I like women."

"So I hear," she said dryly.

He grinned. He was still playing with her hair, which made it hard for her to think. How crazy was that? Her hair? "Have you ever been in love?" she asked.

"No. Have you?"

She started to answer, 'of course' but she stopped before she got the words out. Had she been in love? Really in love? "I thought I was a couple of times," she said, for some reason compelled to be honest. "But when it didn't work out I wasn't sure I ever had been."

"So, you've never been in love either. And now you won't date because you're afraid you're going to be hurt again. Plus, you don't want people to think you're a player."

"Women aren't players," she protested.

"Oh, baby, that's where you're wrong. I've known a number of them."

Come to think of it, so had she. "Okay, I'll concede that point. We don't call them that, usually. More like a flirt or maybe a tease."

"Whatever you want to call them, that's not who you are. It's not who I am either."

He had no idea how much she wanted that to be true. Maybe it was true. Was she so jaded she couldn't trust *any* man to be what he seemed?

"I'm not asking you for a commitment, Samantha. I'm

asking you to give me a chance. That's all. If we have fun, great. If not—" He shrugged. "Then that's that and no hard feelings. Sound like a deal?"

"You never give up, do you?"

He smiled. "Nope. Not when I really want something."

Her breath caught as she looked at him. He wanted her. And damn it, she wanted him right back. But she wasn't quite ready to give in.

"What would this date involve?"

"We could take in a movie, go for a ride, build a snow-man. Go to dinner. Anything you want."

He wouldn't stop pursuing her unless she shut him down entirely. Which, if she were honest with herself, she really didn't want to do. "I have tomorrow off. What if I come out to your place and we go for a ride?"

"That sounds great. What time?"

"Is eleven okay with you?"

"Eleven it is. I'll have Sunshine ready and waiting."

"You've already decided what horse I should ride?"

"I decided that the first time I asked you to come riding. You'll like her. Everyone does." He leaned forward and kissed her cheek. "See you tomorrow." He got out of the car and strode off.

Damn. She was not tingling from a kiss on the cheek. That would be absurd.

Looks like you're absurd then, sister.

"HEY, BOSS, THERE'S a lady asking for you. I put her in the tack room, where it's warm."

Dylan had just finished saddling his gelding, Hawkeye. Leading the horse to the front of the barn, he said, "Thanks, Connor."

"Boss, can I talk to you a minute?"

Dylan stopped. "If you're quick. I don't want to keep the lady waiting."

Connor smiled. "Can't blame you there." He rubbed the bridge of his nose and tipped up his hat, but he seemed to be struggling for words.

"Spit it out," Dylan said.

"That new guy you hired?"

"Jim Monroe? What about him?"

"He don't know much about horses."

"Yeah, I know. He admitted he didn't. But he doesn't need to know anything to muck out a stable. And with Clay out we need the help. Even if it's just grunt work." And now with the cancer diagnosis who knew how long Clay would be unable to work.

"Yeah, but…Burt don't like him."

"Burt likes everyone." Burt was the stable dog who loved horses and horses loved him. Dylan had never known Burt to be anything other than friendly to people, either.

"He don't like Monroe. Burt growled at him."

"Really? That doesn't sound like Burt. Do you know why he growled at him?"

"No, but I thought Monroe was gonna kick him."

"Did he?" That would put a whole different complexion on the matter.

"No, but that's because I showed up before he could. I don't think he likes either dogs or horses. Makes me wonder why he wanted a job here. He's weird, Boss. Always standing around staring and talking to himself."

Dylan resisted the urge to ask what Monroe said when he talked to himself. Maybe he just wasn't that bright. "I can't fire the man because Burt doesn't like him. Tell him to stay away from Burt and I'll talk to him later. Will you saddle Sunshine?"

"For the lady?"

"Yes. The new saddle we got for Mia," he said, speaking of his brother Wyatt's wife.

That conversation didn't bode well for the new employee. Damn it, he'd had a hell of a time finding anyone to hire, period. Much less an experienced ranch hand. He'd had to settle for what he could get. Someone who was inexperienced but willing to take any job.

To tell the truth, Dylan thought there was something a little off about the man too. But he'd claimed to really need the job, and he'd looked down on his luck, so Dylan gave him a chance. Dylan was well aware of his soft spot for anyone or any animal who just needed a break. Usually, it didn't get him into trouble. He'd been wrong about people a time or two, but never about the animals. Which was one reason he was intent on helping Trouble.

He left Hawkeye at the entrance to the barn.

When he opened the tack room door he saw Sam standing with her back to him, looking at the pictures on the walls. "Sorry. I didn't mean to keep you waiting."

Sam turned around and smiled at him. She was bundled up in a down parka, blue jeans and a pair of well-worn cowboy boots. She'd tossed her knit hat and gloves on one of the tables and unzipped her jacket. "That's all right. I was just admiring your photos. Are these all your horses?" she asked, gesturing at the wall of photos.

He walked over to her. "The more recent ones are. The older ones are horses my dad raised."

"Tell me about them."

"My dad raised quarter horses. That first one there was his original stud. He had a fancy name, but we just called him Bucky because he was a buckskin." He continued, pointing out each one and giving a bit of their history. "This is my Fjord stud, Riptide. And the picture next to him is my first Fjord mare, Aria."

"They're beautiful. Their manes are so unusual. They grow that way? White with a black interior? How do they make them look like that? It almost looks like a checkerboard."

"Part of it's natural, part of it's the cut. The distinctive cut of the mane, not to mention the color pattern, are some of the things that set them apart. Their manes stand up unless they're really long, like my new horse's. He hasn't progressed to the stage where we can cut his mane yet." And sometimes Dylan doubted he ever would. "Let's go ride. I'll take you to see all the other horses afterwards, if you want. They're pastured but we'll bring them in a little early because of the weather."

"I'd love to see the horses. Is Sunshine a Fjord?"

"She is. How long has it been since you were on a horse?"

"I haven't ridden since before I left Dallas. Several months ago. But I've been riding since I was four."

"That's right. You mentioned at the party last night that your parents own a ranch."

Connor came in and gave him the thumbs-up sign. "Sunshine is ready and waiting. She's out there with Hawkeye."

"Thanks, Connor."

"Sure, Boss. Want me to check the stirrup length?"

"I think we can handle it," Dylan said dryly.

"Why does he keep smiling like that?" Sam asked after he left.

"I imagine because he thinks you're pretty and wants to hit on you."

She seemed taken aback, then laughed. "Even though I'm here to see you?"

"Connor's never been picky about whose girl he goes after." He opened the door and motioned for her to go out.

"We haven't even had a date. How can I be your girl?" Picking up her hat and gloves, she waited for him to answer.

Dylan gave her a slow smile. "You're not. Yet. But a man can dream."

Chapter Six

I'LL BE GODDAMNED. *It's her. Doctor Samantha Striker. The bitch is here. What in the hell is she doing out here? She works at the hospital. Maybe she came out here to ride. But it's not a stable. It's a horse-breeding ranch. I wonder if she's buying one?*

Standing inside one of the stalls, pretending to muck it out, he watched as the bitch and his boss came out of the tack room, untied their horses and led them out of the barn.

Oh, I get it. Looks like the boss wants some of that. Yeah, she's a looker. He smiled, thinking about his plans for her. *But she won't be pretty once I'm done with her.*

I guess I'll find out if I look as different as I think I do. If she knows who I am when she sees me.

But not yet. Not yet.

First, I'm going to have me some fun with Dr. Samantha Striker. She'll be sorry she fucked with me and mine. Very, very sorry.

A MAN CAN DREAM, Dylan had said. He was smooth, very

much so. But he was sincere. At least, he sure seemed to be sincere.

Sam still wasn't sure why she'd given in to the urge to get to know Dylan better.

Partly because you think he's hot, dumbass.

Sure, that was some of it, but she'd begun to realize there was more to him than the carefree bachelor he was reputed to be. He worked hard. He ran a horse ranch, and from what she'd heard, a successful one. Apparently, though, he still found time to attend to his social life.

He'd said, unnecessarily in her opinion, that he liked women. And women sure as hell liked him. But the very fact that he was still friends with the women he'd dated in the past was significant. According to Bianca, *all* of the women, which made him even more unusual.

Bianca can't possibly know all of them, she reminded herself. Besides, some men were very good at concealing their true nature. She should know.

But all men weren't deceivers like her unlamented ex-boyfriends. Although Sam realized that her experiences had made her more than a little unsure of her judgment where men were concerned.

She was going riding with him. It wasn't a big deal and didn't mean anything. She liked him.

It's a little more than that and you know it. You have the hots for him.

No, I don't. Thinking he's hot and having the hots for him are two different things.

Why was she blowing the whole thing out of proportion?

"Have you finished arguing with yourself?" Dylan asked.

Surprised, she looked at him. "Why do you ask that?"

"It's written all over your face. *I should go. No, I shouldn't. It's not a big deal. But maybe it is. Yes, no, maybe.* What I want to know is what tipped the scales in my favor?"

Sam smiled. "The horses, of course."

Dylan laughed and picked up the reins of a pretty golden-reddish mare with a black and white mane. A red dun, he called her. She nickered when she saw him, nudging him when he came closer. He stroked her nose and looked at Sam. "This is Sunshine. Sunshine, this is Sam." He handed the reins to her and got his own horse to lead the horses out of the barn.

Sam got to know the mare, talking to her, stroking her nose and neck for a bit before she examined the saddle. She checked the girth, the length of the stirrups, the condition of the reins, and the girth again.

She turned to find him watching her. "So, did I pass?"

He laughed. "So far so good."

She grabbed the reins and swung herself up in the saddle.

"Are the stirrups okay?"

She bent down. "They're a little long but I can get them."

He ignored her and shortened them himself. Which, at this point, didn't surprise her. "There, how's that?" he asked.

"Perfect, thanks."

He patted her calf. "It's damn cold today. Are you sure you dressed warmly enough?"

"Yes, long underwear and all."

He gave her a once-over and grinned, but didn't say anything.

"I love her mane. Who did it?" The mare's mane had been cut so that it looked like a fan along the curve of her neck. Predominately white with black hearts at the top every inch or two, it was both whimsical and pretty.

"Clay does it. He's been teaching some of the newer hands to do it but he oversees them." He paused and added, "You should tell him you rode Sunshine when you see him. She's one of his favorites."

"I can see why. She's a sweetie." She watched him walk back to his horse. "Why are you limping?"

"I'm not. Much."

She gave him a disbelieving look.

"It's nothing. My new stallion, Trouble, kicked me in the thigh. I'm usually quick enough to get out of his way but I was distracted. He's the horse that sent Clay to the hospital."

"Did he kick you before or after he sent Clay to the hospital?"

"What difference does that make?"

"So, it was after."

Dylan shrugged and mounted his horse.

"Why do you keep him if he's so dangerous? And if he is,

why don't you geld him?"

"Two reasons. The first is I'm planning on breeding him."

"Even with his temperament?"

"That brings me to my second reason. I don't believe that's his temperament. He was abused. I think he's still scared. That's why he keeps lashing out."

"How long have you been working with him?"

"A few weeks. I've made a little progress, but not much."

"What about your brother?" Having worked with Sean, who was an ER doc, for some time now, Sam remembered several conversations she'd had with him or overheard about Sean's way with horses. "Haven't I heard Sean is a horse whisperer?"

"Yeah, but even Sean hasn't been able to get through to him. Although, Trouble didn't bite him, so that's progress, I guess. Enough about Trouble. Are you ready to go?"

"Absolutely." And she was ridiculously excited about being on a horse again. It had been way too long.

IT DIDN'T TAKE too long for Dylan to relax. Sam obviously knew what she was doing, regardless of the fact she hadn't ridden in quite a while. She and Sunshine were getting along fine. Sam looked comfortable in the saddle and from what he could tell in such a short amount of time, she wasn't going to have any problems riding.

The day was crisp and cold, the sky clear and blue, the company perfect. Sam didn't chatter. She seemed fine with simply enjoying the ride. He pointed out Lovers' Creek and a few other points of interest, but mostly left her to her thoughts.

"I've really missed this," she said. "Thank you."

"You're welcome. Why haven't you gone out to the Canadays' place to ride? You've been here several months."

"I don't know. The time never seemed right and honestly, I was afraid it would make me miss my mare, Greta, more than I already did."

"Is she with your parents?"

"No. She passed a couple of months before I moved. From old age. But it's still hard."

"It sucks."

"It surely does. This sweetheart is making me realize I shouldn't have cut myself off from all horses. I'm not sure it didn't make things worse."

"You're welcome to ride any time you want. Sunshine or another—" Dylan broke off and came to a standstill. "Do you hear that? It sounds like a dog whimpering."

"Yes. It's getting louder." She twisted around in the saddle. "I can't tell where it's coming from. Can you?"

"Not yet." They both scanned the surroundings looking for the source of the noise. "There. I think it's coming from that stand of trees." He rode over to it. Beneath an overhang of branches, lying in the snow, clearly exhausted, was a medium-sized black dog. He dismounted and walked over to the dog, squatting down beside it. "Hey, fella." *Goddamn it, another dog dumped in the country.* Possibly a stray but more likely someone had deliberately dumped him. It happened all the time.

He studied the ground, trying to figure out why the dog had stopped where he was. Three paw prints, two front and one hind, gave him a good idea. Very gently, he ran his hands over the dog, who yelped when he touched his right rear leg, but didn't offer to bite him.

"What's wrong? Is it hurt?" Sam dismounted, walked over to them and knelt down in the snow. The dog wagged its tail weakly.

"I think he might have a broken leg. Plus, he's shivering. He could be hypothermic." He stood, stripped off his coat and handed it to Sam.

"What are you doing? It's freezing."

"Yeah, I know. So is he." He picked up the dog, who yelped again but was too tired to struggle, and said, "Help me wrap that coat around him. I'm going to put him up on my saddle and take him back."

"You're crazy," she said, but she helped steady the dog on the saddle as Dylan mounted Hawkeye. "You'll be lucky if *you* don't get hypothermia."

"Nah, we won't be out that long. We're walking, though. I'm afraid anything else will jar him too much. Sorry to cut short the ride."

"Don't be ridiculous," she said.

Chapter Seven

"NOW I KNOW why you have so many dogs," Sam said as they rode back. "You must keep all of them."

He shot her a wry glance. "Hardly. I find homes for a lot of them."

"And the ones you can't find a home for, you keep."

"I live on a ranch. There's plenty of room. But it really pisses me off when people dump them."

"My parents have that problem too. Although they don't have nearly as many dogs as you do. One of the hazards of living in the country." She thought about the dogs she'd seen. Six? Eight? "How many do you have, anyway?"

"Now? Or generally? It tends to change."

"How many dogs are yours that you aren't trying to find a home for?"

"I don't know. It varies. They mostly live outside, but there's an open stall with hay in the barn, where they go when the weather's bad. Right now I have Burt—he runs the place. I've had him a long time. He keeps all the other dogs in line. Loves the horses. They all like horses, but Burt is the head honcho. Anyway, then there's Sugar, Mike, Ike, Spike, Rosa and... Oh, yeah, Rita. Who wouldn't appreciate me forgetting her. How many is that? Seven?"

"Yes, seven. That's a lot of dogs."

"Could be eight, depending on what happens with Shadow, here."

She didn't miss the considering look he gave her. "Shadow? You named him already?"

"We can change it if you don't like that."

"Why would I have any say—" She broke off and stared at him.

"You like dogs, don't you?"

"Yes, but—"

"Do you have one?"

"No, but—"

"He's a sweetheart. Even if his leg isn't broken, he's injured. He didn't even snap at me when I moved him. He just whimpered."

"Oh, Dylan, I can't." But she found herself looking at the dog and wondering if she could manage.

"Why not?"

"For one thing, I have such odd hours. It wouldn't be fair to him... Would it?"

Dylan smiled as they reached the stable. "We'll talk about it. Connor, Bret, Jim," he yelled, "I need some help here."

Shortly, two men came out from the barn. Dylan had

dismounted and started carrying the dog to the barn, leading his horse. Sam dismounted and followed Dylan.

"Can you two take care of the horses?" Dylan asked.

"Sure thing, Boss," Connor said.

"Where's Jim?"

"Haven't seen him since this morning," Connor said. "Not that he'd be and help—"

Dylan cut him off. "Never mind. I'll talk to him later."

"Where did you find that one?" the other man asked.

"Near Lovers' Creek. I don't know what it is about that place but more stray dogs show up there than anywhere else." To Sam he said, "I don't usually let anyone else cool down the horses but I need to get the dog warm right away. I'm going to take him up to the house."

"Do you want me to help with the horses or the dog?" Sam asked.

"Whichever you want."

Since the two men were obviously capable of caring for the horses, she went with Dylan up to the house.

Sam opened the kitchen door for Dylan, who walked in calling, "Glory! Hey, Glory, where are you?" He walked over to the fireplace and took a seat close to the hearth with the dog still in his arms.

A small, slim woman who looked to be in her late fifties bustled in. "What in the world is the matter?" Catching sight of the dog, she parked her hands on her hips. "Dylan Gallagher, have you brought home *another* dog?"

Far from seeming chastened, Dylan smiled at her. "Found him by the creek. I need some warm blankets, Glory. He's pretty cold."

She sniffed, but seemed resigned. "Since Dylan has forgotten his manners, I'm Glory, the housekeeper."

"I'm Samantha," she said to Glory's back as she went into another room off the kitchen.

Shortly, Glory came back with blankets in her arms. Together they helped Dylan unwrap his coat from around the dog and wrap him in a blanket. "I'll warm up some broth and we'll mix it with the dog food." Glory said. "Poor thing. Can I get you something, Samantha? Coffee? Hot chocolate? Water?"

"I would love some hot chocolate, if it's not too much trouble." Normally, Sam drank coffee or water, but the hot chocolate sounded like it would hit the spot.

"Sam's one of the trauma surgeons at the hospital," Dylan said. "And I'll take a cup of coffee, please."

"Oh, then you must know my other boys," Glory said.

Sam bit her lip at the description of the Gallagher men as Glory's 'boys'. "Yes, I know Jack, Sean and Wyatt. I've worked with all of them."

"What got into you to take off your coat, Dylan?" Glory asked. "You'll be lucky if you don't catch your death."

"Glory worries too much," he told Sam.

She sat beside Dylan and reached beneath the blanket to pat the dog's head. "He's looking better already."

"I think he'll be okay once we get some food and water into him. And have him checked out by a vet."

"I'll go get some dog food," Glory said, adding on her way out of the kitchen, "There's peach cobbler if you're hungry."

"I'll take a rain check. I've got my hands full right now. As soon as he's warm I'm going to run him into town to see Matt West. You should eat some cobbler, though," Dylan told Sam. "Glory is a great cook."

"I can wait," Sam said. "What can I do?"

"Here," Dylan said, plopping the dog, blankets and all, in her lap. "I'll get some water for him." He disappeared in the same direction Glory had.

"He's not very subtle, is he?" she asked the dog. "You know, Shadow is a good name for you." Shadow raised his head and perked up his ears. Sam sighed and scratched his head. "I wonder if I'll regret this?"

"Regret what?" Dylan asked. He put a water dish on the floor. "Let's see if he'll drink some."

Sam unwrapped him and put him down beside the water dish. He sniffed at the bowl, then stood, favoring the injured leg, and lapped up some water. "Don't let him drink too much at first," Sam cautioned.

Dylan grinned and removed the water after the dog drank some. "Regret what?" he asked again.

"You know very well, what. Don't try to act innocent."

"It's not an act," he told her, with an injured expression.

"I am innocent."

Glory came in just then and burst out laughing. Looking at Sam, she said, "Oh, honey, if you believe that I have some prime swampland to sell you."

IT HAD BEEN one of those days, at least so far. After taking his temperature several times, they decided Shadow was doing well enough to go to the vet. Sam went out to her car to lay down a blanket on the back seat. She tried to start the car to warm it up, but after several tries, she finally admitted defeat. Glory said Dylan was in the barn getting some tools together so she went to find him.

"I've got problems," she said when she found him. One of Dylan's ranch hands had been with him but he left as soon as he saw her heading that way. "I'd ask if it was it something I said, but I hadn't even spoken."

"What, Jim? I wouldn't worry about him. He's new and—" dropping his voice, he added with a shrug "—kind of weird. But with Clay out for who knows how long, I needed more help. So, what's the problem?"

"My car won't start."

"Did you look under the hood?"

"Why would I do that? I'm a doctor, not a mechanic."

"Good point." He laughed and followed her to the car. He got in, turned the key, and he couldn't get it started either. Sam expected him to get out and look at the engine but he stayed where he was, looking at the dashboard. "I think I see your problem."

"Already? What is it?"

"You're out of gas. It's below empty. I don't know how you managed to get here. You must have been running on fumes."

Sam frowned and knit her brows. "I may be a dummy about cars, but I know enough to put gas in it. I filled up a couple of days ago. I shouldn't be out."

"Are you sure it was just a couple of days ago? Maybe it's been longer."

"I'm positive. That's so weird."

"You must have a leak. I've got gas here. I can give you enough to get to town and to a mechanic. Unless the leak is so bad we have to have it towed."

"Great," she muttered. Luckily, though, the car started after Dylan put gas in it and didn't show signs of a leak initially. She should have felt stupid. She suspected Dylan still thought she'd forgotten but she knew for a fact she'd had at least a quarter of a tank when she drove out to the ranch. A quarter of a tank that had mysteriously disappeared.

Dylan loaded Shadow into his truck and followed her to drop off her car and then go to Matt West's veterinary office.

Dr. West checked the dog for a chip, but didn't find one, which didn't surprise anyone. He said Shadow's leg wasn't broken, but found a jagged tear likely caused by Shadow tangling with a barbwire fence. Since it was on the inside of his leg, high on the flank, and his hair had been so badly matted, Sam and Dylan hadn't found it when they'd examined him. Not to mention that getting him warm had been their first priority.

Dr. West suggested they leave him until later in the afternoon so that he could finish examining him. He would stitch up his wound, clean him up and give him his shots. He said to bring him back if he didn't improve in a few days. Otherwise, once Shadow was well enough the doctor would neuter him.

Sam and Dylan then went to pick up food, a bed and other things she thought she'd need as a new dog owner. They stopped at another store to get the doggie door and then they went to her house.

Who knew I was so...shallow? Sam wondered, watching Dylan working on her kitchen door later that afternoon. *It's not as if I've never seen a male backside.*

Not that fine, you haven't.

"You really didn't have to stay," she said. "I can get someone to bring the car to me when they're finished." She'd also argued that he didn't need to install the door, much less pay for it, but he'd ignored her. He'd been working for what seemed like hours.

Dylan turned around to look at her. "That makes the fourth or fifth time you've said that to me. What's going on? Do you want me to leave?"

"No, of course not. I feel guilty because you're having to

do all this to my house."

"All this? You mean put in a doggie door? That's no big deal."

"It's taking forever. And you paid for it. You also checked my fence to make sure there weren't any holes in it."

"That wasn't hard either. Besides, I figure I owe it to you since I persuaded you to take Shadow home."

"That's true. You do."

He smiled and put in the last screw. "Now you'll be able to leave him while you work and not feel guilty about keeping him cooped up."

"I've always heard doggie doors are an invitation to burglars. Luckily, there isn't a lot of crime here in Marietta."

"Not that I've heard of. But then, I live in the country. We don't even lock our doors."

"I'm still far too big-city for that. I'm glad I have the next couple of days off. I want to make sure Shadow feels at home."

"Don't worry. I bet he will. I'll clean up and then we can see if your car is ready."

She helped him pick up the pieces of wood and sweep up the shavings, then load his tools into his truck. "Do you have to get back right away? After we pick up my car, I mean."

"Why? Is there something else you want me to do?"

"Stay for dinner."

He looked surprised. "I'd like that. Let me call the ranch and see if they need me. As far as I know there shouldn't be anything they can't handle."

She hadn't intended to ask Dylan to dinner. But then, she hadn't meant to spend all day with him either. One thing led to another, and she had needed his help getting ready to keep Shadow. Feeding him was the least she could do after all he'd done.

Yes, and it has nothing to do with not wanting the day to end. Nope, not a thing.

Chapter Eight

DYLAN OFFERED TO pick up Shadow and meet Sam at her house after he dropped her off to pick up the car. She tried to give him money for the vet, but he wouldn't let her pay for that either.

"My God, you're stubborn," she said to Dylan.

"I have to be. I'm the youngest of five kids."

"You really won't let me pay for the vet?"

"Afraid not."

"I give up."

"That's the plan."

She didn't quite slam the door when she got out of his truck at the auto repair shop.

"Was there a hole in the gas tank?" she asked the mechanic.

"No. Everything looks good."

"Then how did I run out of gas so completely? I swear I filled it up."

The mechanic shrugged. "I couldn't find anything to indicate it was leaking gas." He rubbed his chin. "Could someone have siphoned off your gas?"

"Siphoned off my gas? Why would anyone do that?"

"Dunno." He shrugged. "Maybe they didn't have any money and needed gas."

"Maybe, but it still seems weird. Besides, I don't know when they'd have done it." Could that be the answer? What a strange thing to happen.

She and Dylan arrived at her house at almost the same time, so she didn't have a chance to tell him about the car immediately. She put Shadow's new bed in the kitchen by his food and water, thinking she could move the bed from room to room. Shadow sniffed around the room, then, satisfied with whatever he'd smelled, he went to his pillow, turned a couple of circles and settled down with a sigh. Already a little in love with him, Sam sat beside him and petted him, promising him a treat after dinner.

"So what happened with your car?" Dylan asked.

Sam stood and went to the sink to wash her hands. "It's the weirdest thing. The mechanic couldn't find a gas leak anywhere. He said the car was in good shape. When I told him I'd filled up recently he asked if someone could have siphoned off the gas."

"Yeah, I guess that could be it. That happened more often when the price of gas was really high, though."

"I know. It seems like such a random thing to happen."

"If that's the case, when would they have done it? Did you have gas when you got to the ranch this morning?"

"I thought I did, but honestly, I probably didn't check."

"Where have you been since you filled up? Do you know?"

"Too many places to count. My place, your place, the hospital, the parking lot downtown. I'm sure there are others. I can't remember all of them."

"I guess that's not much help then. Except that does sound like the most likely explanation."

"So I'll never know when or where it happened."

"Doesn't sound like it. Do you want to report it?"

"Report it to who? The cops? I think they have more important things on their minds than someone stealing a few gallons of gas." That was that. No point in worrying about something there was no way of tracing.

"I'm going to start dinner." Earlier she'd thawed out a lasagna she'd cooked and frozen a few weeks before, during one of her cooking marathons. "I hope you like lasagna," she said, taking the dish out of the refrigerator and setting it on the stovetop.

"Love it."

Startled, she turned to find Dylan behind her.

"What can I do?" he asked. "Do you want me to set the table?"

"Okay, but it's going to take a little while to heat the lasagna." She turned the oven on convection to speed up the process, then got out the silverware and handed it to him. "The last time I microwaved lasagna it did not turn out well.

Besides, I think the microwave is broken."

"I'd offer to see what I could do to fix it," he said while laying out knives, forks and napkins, "but if mine doesn't work I just buy a new one."

"That would probably be easier than being chained here waiting on a repairman. Unfortunately, this one is built in so it isn't that easy to replace."

Opening the refrigerator again, she pulled out salad fixings. "Would you like a glass of wine? I'm sorry, but I don't have any beer."

"Wine sounds good."

Sam handed him the bottle and a corkscrew and got out two wine glasses. While he took care of that, she finished the salad and put it back in the refrigerator. Dylan poured the wine and gave her a glass. Tapping his glass to hers, he said, "To Shadow and his new home with you."

After toasting, Sam said, "We could go into the living room while we wait."

"We could." Dylan set down his glass, took hers and set it beside his. Framing her face with his hands, he said, "I've been wanting to do this since the first time I laid eyes on you." And then he kissed her.

Her lips parted of their own volition. His tongue slipped inside her mouth, coaxing hers to answer. Her mind blanked, but her body responded. Hesitantly at first but then she relaxed and simply enjoyed kissing a man who really knew how to kiss.

He lifted his head and smiled at her. "Are you this cautious with everyone or is it just me?"

"Both."

He dropped his hands but he didn't move away. "Why?"

She answered honestly. "I'm cautious with everyone because of past experience. But with you—" she hesitated then finished "—I have a feeling that if I get involved with you it won't be something easily forgotten, or something easily walked away from." And she wasn't at all sure she was ready for that.

"I suspect you're right. Too late, though. We're already involved."

"Are we?"

Flicking a finger under her chin, he said, "Maybe you aren't but I sure as hell am."

She stared at him, unable to think of how to respond. Was he right? Was it too late because they were both involved already? He didn't seem to expect her to say anything. He picked up his glass and took a sip, then set it down again. "How about some music?"

Sam breathed a sigh of relief. Or disappointment. She couldn't be sure which one. "Okay. Did you have something in mind?"

He pulled his cell phone out of his pocket. "I have some music on my phone."

She was curious to know what kind of music he liked. Shortly, the mellow sounds of a piano issued from his phone.

"That's beautiful," Sam said. "Who is it? It sounds classical."

"It is, in a way. Some call it new age and some call it contemporary classical. I just call it beautiful. It's by Yiruma. He's a South Korean composer."

"What's the name of this song?"

"'The River Flows In You'." He set down the phone and picked up his wine.

"I wouldn't have thought you were a classical music buff." A cowboy classical music aficionado. Interesting.

He grinned at her over his wine glass. "Because I'm a rancher?"

"Well, yes. I didn't mean to stereotype. But you have to admit, country western music would be more common." But then, Dylan Gallagher was anything but ordinary.

He shrugged. "I like country. I also like classical, new age, rock, pop, jazz, and rap. And I listen to hip-hop, alternative, salsa, bluegrass and gospel, too, though not as much as the others. I like all kinds of music."

"That's quite a list. You have extremely eclectic tastes. Is there any genre you don't like?"

"Probably, but I try to keep an open mind. I have my favorites, though. This is one of them."

The music changed to another instrumental piece. "Who is this?"

"Philip Wesley. 'Dark Night of the Soul'."

"It's beautiful. Do you know every song on your playlist?"

"On this one, I do. But I have a lot of playlists and don't always know the particular song. I can generally recognize the composer if it's someone like Mozart or Beethoven."

She laughed. "Finally, music even I might be able to recognize." She drank some wine. "As much as you like music I'm surprised you don't play an instrument."

He chuckled, leaning back against the counter and taking another sip of wine. "I have no talent. Jack plays the guitar and he tried to teach me, but that didn't work. After that I tried piano, French horn, saxophone and violin. Every single one a bust. My dad was really worried I'd leave the ranch to be some kind of musician. Until about the third instrument and he realized that would never happen."

"But he still let you try other instruments?"

"He promised our mother that he would encourage all of us to play an instrument. Glenna played piano. Jack and Glenna are the only ones who have any musical talent."

"Glenna's your sister?"

For a moment, his expression clouded. "Yes. She's closest to me in age. Only a year older."

The timer dinged and Sam took the lasagna out of the oven. Leaving it to sit a moment, she microwaved some frozen vegetables and set out the salad bowl. The microwave had good and bad days and she could only hope this was one of its good ones. "Dig in," she told him when everything was ready. They served themselves and took their plates to the table. One song gave way to another gorgeous instrumental piece that she didn't recognize.

"Did you make this yourself?" Dylan asked after tasting it.

"Yes, why?"

"It's really good. Better than Glory's. But if you tell her I said that I'll call you a liar."

Sam laughed. "Don't worry. Your secret is safe with me."

"Good. If Glory didn't cook for me I'd probably starve."

"I certainly wouldn't want that on my conscience. What got you started with classical music?"

"My mother."

"I thought you said she passed away when you were six?"

"She did. But we kept her cassette tapes and player and a lot of them were classical music. I listened to them all the time. My brothers thought I was weird, but Glenna understood."

"She doesn't live here, does she?" Since she'd never heard anything about the Gallagher sister, she assumed she lived elsewhere.

"No. She was working on a cattle ranch in Argentina until a few weeks ago. She—" He broke off, as if searching for words. "She disappeared and we haven't been able to find her."

Sam put a hand on his arm, giving it a gentle squeeze. "I'm sorry. That must be hard."

He acknowledged it with a jerky nod. "We hired a private investigator but he hasn't had any luck so far."

"How long has he been searching?"

"About three weeks, but we were told she'd been gone for months by the time Dylan called. When Hardeman, that's the PI—went down to the ranch in Argentina he discovered that was a lie. She'd only been gone a couple of weeks. Even so, the PI doesn't seem much closer to finding her. We don't know why her employers lied about timing, either." Shrugging, he said, "Enough about my family. Do you have brothers or sisters?"

Accepting the change of subject, she said, "One of each. They both live in Texas. My brother is a doctor too. He lives in Houston. My sister is in marketing for a large company in San Antonio. I miss them. Even though we lived in different parts of Texas we still saw each other fairly often."

"Your entire family is in Texas?" She nodded. "You sound like you're close to them. What made you move so far away?"

Bianca was the only person who knew the real reason she'd left Dallas. It wasn't something she talked about. "It's a long story," she said after a long moment.

"Which you don't want to talk about."

"I doubt it's anything you'd want to hear."

"Anything you want to talk about is fine with me. But if you don't want to talk, that's okay too." He got up and started to clear the table.

"You don't need to do that."

"Sure I do. You cooked. I'll clean up."

"You're not doing it alone."

After they cleaned up Sam took Shadow out. Dylan came outside with them and together they watched him. "He's still limping but not as much as he was before the vet saw him. He looks like he's patrolling the yard," Sam said.

"He does. I get the feeling he's going to be very protective of you."

Sam laughed. "I don't imagine I'll need him to be, but it is kind of comforting."

After Shadow finished they went back inside. Sam got Shadow settled in his bed and gave him a chew toy. She stood watching him for a moment, her back to Dylan. "I lost a patient."

The sudden confession didn't faze him. "I'm sorry. Recently?"

"No. When I was in Dallas. It's why I left."

"Was it the first patient you lost?"

"No. I work in an ER. I'm going to lose patients. It's a fact of life."

"But this one was different."

She nodded, wondering why she was telling him such a grim story. But there was something about Dylan that made her want to confide in him. Something that made her feel safe. That made her feel that she could trust him not to judge her, no matter what she told him. "Losing a patient is always bad but the way she died made it even worse." She raised her head and looked into his eyes. "She was murdered.

Shot to death in front of me."

SIPHONING THE GAS *from her car had been the perfect kickoff to his plan. Start slow and build up, he told himself. Don't rush it. Even if she figures out what happened, she won't know where or when it happened. Go slow. At first. But later…he wanted her scared. Nervous. Wondering what the hell was going to happen next. Wondering if it was just bad luck…or something else. Something worse.*

It was obvious the boss had the hots for her. So she'd be coming out to the ranch more often. He would have to think of something new for the next time she did. Unless he could find out where she lived. Shouldn't be too hard…

Chapter Nine

FOR A MOMENT she faltered. But it had been well over a year since the shooting had taken place and while the desire to bury what had happened was strong, the need to talk about it was stronger.

"Her husband shot her. And then he shot me."

Dylan put his hand on her shoulder and gave it a comforting squeeze. "I'm sorry doesn't really cut it, but it's all I have. How badly were you hurt?"

"An inch closer to my heart and I wouldn't be here talking to you. But I lived. And in a deposition from my hospital bed I was able to give my testimony that sent him to jail for life."

"I'm glad you were able to have him put away, but it's not much consolation for losing a patient. Or a friend. Not to mention nearly losing your own life."

Amber had been a friend as well as a patient. Dylan had picked up on that. "No, it's not."

"Let's sit down," Dylan said, steering her to the couch and sitting beside her.

"Are you sure you want to hear this? It's not exactly a lighthearted conversation."

Dylan reached for her hand and held it. "You wouldn't have mentioned it at all if you weren't ready to talk about it."

He was right about that. And even though they didn't know each other well, she thought Dylan would be a good person to talk to. Objective, yet compassionate. "Bianca knows but we don't talk about it. Not anymore. We haven't in a long time. I keep thinking I've put it behind me, that I've dealt with it, but…"

"I don't imagine many people are able to completely get over something so traumatic."

"All I know is I haven't. I want to but then something will happen to remind me and I question myself all over again. Was it my fault? What could I have done differently? But there's never a good answer."

"You sound like you feel responsible for what happened."

"I do. I am responsible. Her husband found her because of me."

"She was hiding from him?"

"Yes. I met Amber Baxter when her husband, Gary, brought her into the ER one night. They told the usual story. She'd fallen down the stairs. She had a broken arm, a couple of broken ribs, a black eye. I knew he'd done it. I not only worked the ER but I was heavily involved with a local women's shelter. So I knew.

"I managed to get her alone when she had X-rays. This

was far from her first hospital trip and she was desperate to get away from him. Like most women, she was terrified of her abuser. Certain he'd kill her if she left him." Sam laughed without humor. "I'd heard it before and I knew the most dangerous time for an abused woman is when she tries to leave her abuser. While I didn't discount what she'd said, I thought we'd be able to help her before he got to her. If I had taken her more seriously, she might still be alive."

"You can't know that," Dylan said. "What would you have done differently? Would changing how you went about helping her have changed the outcome?"

"I don't know." She rubbed her free hand over her eyes. "Probably not."

"But you still beat yourself up over it. Even though you did what you thought best at the time."

"Yes." She probably always would.

"Sam." He squeezed her hand comfortingly. "You had no way of knowing what would happen."

"I know. But I still feel guilty."

"That's normal in this type of situation. Don't you think?"

He was so kind. So understanding. So completely non-judgmental. "That's what Bianca thinks. She says I'm harder on myself than anyone else would ever be."

He smiled a little. "You should listen to Bianca. She's right."

"Maybe." She sighed, wishing she could be as sure as

Bianca and Dylan were that Amber's death wasn't her fault. "I convinced Amber to bring charges against him and to come to the shelter that night, after she left the hospital. When the cops came to take her husband away, he went crazy, threatening to kill Amber, me and anyone else who had helped her. It wasn't anything I hadn't heard before. He might have been more volatile than the others, but I'd seen a lot of extremely angry men. Amber moved into the shelter that night. Though Gary didn't go to jail, she was able to get a restraining order against him. So many women go back to their abusers. For as many reasons as there are women. But Amber didn't. She worked hard at getting her life together without him. She'd have made it too."

"If her husband hadn't killed her," Dylan said.

"Yes. It still haunts me. I wonder if I'll ever learn to accept it."

"Why do you think you were responsible for her death?"

"I told you, he found her through me. While the ultimate responsibility is his, I made it easier for him. He started following me. I didn't realize it and led him to the shelter. He must have known or guessed I'd helped Amber find a place to live. Somewhere we thought she'd be safe from him. He watched the place for days, until one day he got lucky and found Amber and me together on the front porch. He shot Amber and while I was trying to stop the bleeding, he shot me."

Dylan put his arm around her and gave her a comforting

hug. "It's not your fault, Sam."

"Then why does it feel like it is?" she mumbled against his shirt. She slipped her arm around his waist and rested her head against his shoulder. She could feel the empathy flowing from him, washing over her, soothing her, relieving some of her pain.

"Because you're trying to make sense of something that's incomprehensible."

DYLAN WASN'T PARTICULARLY happy about the reason he was sitting on Sam's couch holding her in his arms, but he liked the result. Too soon, she sat up and moved away. She tilted her head, studying him.

"What?" he asked her. "You've got a strange look on your face."

"I'm wondering why in the world I told you that awful story. I'm usually much more of a private person."

"Must be something about my face. Sometimes I think I should have been a bartender."

She smiled. "I take it a lot of people confide in you."

"A few," he admitted.

Sam lifted an eyebrow.

"Okay, some. More than some, but less than a lot," he amended.

"Is there a word for that?"

"No, but we could make one up."

She smiled again, then turned serious. "Thank you. I hope I didn't make you too uncomfortable."

He stared at her. "Good God, Sam, you're the one who was shot, nearly died and lost a friend."

"Still. We don't even know each other that well and here I am dumping a terrible story on you. I shouldn't have done it. But you're so easy to talk to I did it anyway."

"I think it's a sign that we should get to know each other better."

"Do you? And how do you propose we do that?"

Somehow he didn't think she'd go for what he thought was the best way to get to know each other.

"No."

"I didn't say anything."

"You didn't have to. It was written all over your face."

"See, you know me better than you thought."

"No, I don't. I just know men."

"Ouch." Dylan patted his chest. "An arrow to the heart."

"That's your sternum you're patting, not your heart."

Dylan laughed. "Why don't you come out to the ranch again and I'll introduce you to the horses and show you around. We didn't manage it this time since we had to take care of Shadow." He glanced over at the dog. "I hope snoring doesn't bother you."

"I'm sure I'll get used to it. I'd love to see the horses but I don't know when that will be. I don't want to leave Shadow for a long period until I have to."

"Bring him with you."

"The vet said to keep him calm and don't let him do much for a few days."

"Oh, yeah. I forgot about that." He stood, reached for her hand and pulled her up beside him. "We'll do it once Shadow is better. In the meantime, do you have plans for tomorrow night?"

"Other than taking care of Shadow, no. Why?"

"Let me bring dinner over."

She hesitated for a moment. He wondered what was going on in her head. Then she smiled and said, "I'd like that. What are you going to pick up?"

"I'll get Glory to make something."

"She doesn't need to go to that trouble."

"Glory's a romantic. She'll be happy to do it."

"Is that what this is? A romance?"

He let go of her hand and traced his fingers down her jawline and then over her lips. "I sure as hell hope so." He kissed her, slow and easy. She tasted faintly of wine, but with a flavor that was all her own. He deepened the kiss, but held back from what he really wanted to do. He wanted her melting in his arms, pliant against him, wanted her breasts in his hands, wanted skin against skin, her hips cradling him, welcoming him.

She put her arms around his neck and kissed him back, but he felt her hesitancy to give in fully to what was between them. He lifted his mouth from hers and smiled at her before releasing her. "I'll see you tomorrow night," he said. Then he got the hell out of there before he took things to their logical conclusion. One she clearly wasn't ready for yet.

SAM DIDN'T SLEEP particularly well that night. Not because of Shadow. She brought his pillow into the bedroom and he immediately fell asleep and slept like a baby all night. A baby who snored. But she didn't mind. Having a dog was comforting. She'd had dogs growing up but not since she left home. Her schedule had always been too difficult for her to have a pet.

But now the hospital wasn't more than a few minutes away. She was rarely so busy that she couldn't come home for a short time to check on the dog. Remembering how he'd laid his head in her lap and looked at her with those big, brown, puppy dog eyes—she was falling for him already.

And what about Dylan? Are you falling for him too?

Crap. Of course she was. If she'd been just a tiny bit more impulsive she'd had been in bed with Dylan two minutes after that kiss.

And what's wrong with that?

"Stop it," she said aloud. She fluffed up her pillow, lay back down and tried to sleep. But it was a long time coming. And when she finally fell asleep she dreamed of—who else?—Dylan Gallagher.

Whose damn dog is barking? Sam sat up, rubbing her eyes. A glance at the clock showed seven a.m. The barking dog, she realized, was hers. Shadow was barking madly at the front door.

Oh, shit. I forgot about Bianca. In lieu of a robe, which she didn't own, she pulled on a sweatshirt over her T-shirt and flannel pants and went to answer the door.

"When did you get a dog?" Bianca asked immediately. She held out the back of her hand to Shadow, who sniffed and wagged his tail, apparently signifying his approval of their guest.

"Yesterday. Obviously, I forgot we were running. Do you want coffee?"

"Does a bear shit in the woods?"

"I've never seen one doing it. Have you?" She led the way to the kitchen and turned on the coffee maker she'd prepared the night before.

"No, but they're bound to. So, where did you get the dog? He's awfully skinny. Is he a stray? Did you get him from the shelter? What's his name?"

"His name is Shadow. I'll tell you all about it once I've got my coffee." She opened the back door and let Shadow out, watching him from the doorway. His limp was already better, even just since yesterday, though he still strongly favored his injured leg.

"I couldn't figure out why you'd bailed on me without calling," Bianca said.

"I totally forgot. Sorry." Sam fixed a bowl of food for Shadow. By then the coffee was ready, and she poured them both a mug, setting Bianca's down in front of her. "He's a stray. Dylan found him out at the Gallagher ranch and I wound up offering to take care of him."

"How did that happen? Did Dylan just call you up and say, 'Hey, I found a stray. Want him?'"

Sam rolled her eyes. "I was with him when he found him. We were riding."

"Aha! You gave in. About time. I figured you would after I saw you two together at my birthday party. You left at the same time, too. Did you two spend the night together?"

"No, and what's with the inquisition? We talked about horses and one thing led to another. I went out to his ranch to ride the next morning and that's when we found the dog."

"When are you seeing him again?"

"Tonight."

Bianca whistled, causing Shadow, who was lying at Sam's feet, to prick up his ears. "Sounds like things are heating up."

Sam didn't answer that directly. "You know my track record with men. I always go for the wrong guys."

"I've already told you, Dylan's a good guy."

"That's what I thought about the others."

"Would it help you to know I never slept with Dylan?"

Sam looked at her closely. Bianca wouldn't lie about something like that. "Why didn't you?"

"We didn't date long, and it was very casual. We liked each other but neither of us was that involved. I don't think I'm the only woman he's gone out with who he hasn't slept with."

Maybe it was unreasonable of her, but knowing that did

make her feel better. "He's easy to be with. Easy to talk to. I told him about Dallas," she added. "I don't know why I did. He asked me why I left Texas since I was obviously close to my family. The whole story about Amber just came out."

Bianca was staring at her with her mouth open. "I didn't think you ever talked about that."

"I don't. That's why it was so strange that I told Dylan."

"How did he react?"

"He was sympathetic. He told me it wasn't my fault and that I was trying to make sense of something that was incomprehensible."

"He's right about that."

"There's a women's shelter in Billings," Sam said. "You volunteer there, don't you?"

Bianca nodded. "Not a lot, but they're grateful for any help I can offer."

"I've thought about it," Sam said. "But I just can't do it. Does that make me a coward? I know that what happened is the exception and not the norm. But I can't make myself volunteer."

Bianca reached out and squeezed her hand. "I doubt many people could after what you went through. Don't beat yourself up over it. You do a lot to help people as it is. There's no need to put yourself through something that would be so traumatic for you."

But if I don't face my fears will I ever be able to truly put the past behind me?

Chapter Ten

THE NEXT MORNING Sean came out to help Dylan with Trouble. But when they took him out to the round pen the stallion scorned Sean's attempts to bond with him. He didn't bite or kick him, which Dylan saw as progress. But he wasn't having any of Sean's magic way with horses.

"I don't know what to tell you, Dylan. I don't get the feeling he's mean. He reacts out of fear, but I don't know how to reach him."

"He's gotten a little better with me. He'll let me brush him and pick out his hooves. He wouldn't do that at first. He still won't let me do anything to his mane, except brush it occasionally. That's progress, I guess. But damn, it's slow going."

"He's a beauty."

Dylan didn't often question his decisions about horses but he was beginning to get worried that he'd made a mistake. "Do you think I'm crazy to keep trying?"

Sean rubbed the back of his neck. "Not necessarily. How is Riptide doing? How badly do you need another stud?"

His original Fjord stud was the backbone of his breeding program. But if he wanted to expand he needed at least one more stud. "Riptide is good. He's got a lot of years left. But I'd like another bloodline too."

"Not a bad idea. If he doesn't work out are you going to sell Trouble?"

"No." He wouldn't trust anyone else not to mistreat the horse. Especially given how difficult he was. "I've thought about gelding him. But damn, I'd hate to do that. He could be a great stud."

"Yeah, if you can teach him not to put people in the hospital. And speaking of that, I hear Clay is going home soon. When does he start chemo?"

"Jack wants him to be more recovered from his injuries before he starts. You know how hard chemo can be on the immune system."

"Yeah, I know."

Dylan knew Sean was thinking of their mother, just as he was. But it was even worse for Sean because he'd been a teenager when their mother died, so he remembered a lot more about their mother's cancer than Dylan did. "I've lined up some help for him when he gets home. Glory found her, actually. She'll be able to take him to and from his treatments and do whatever else he needs."

"That's good. I'm kind of surprised he's agreed to it."

Dylan grinned. "He hasn't. He doesn't know anything about it yet."

"Damn. Who's going to tell him?"

"Jack's his doctor. I'm leaving all that up to him."

"Good plan."

"How's Honey?" Dylan asked, speaking of Sean's wife.

"She's great. She has a barrel race this weekend. She's been killing it lately."

"Are you going?"

"Yes, I'm off work." Sean put a boot up on the rail. "We've been talking about having a kid."

Dylan joined him, looking at him with amusement. "I have it on good authority that's not how you get them."

"Ha ha. You're a riot. With Jack and Maya having Will, and Wyatt and Mia due in a few months, it's no wonder Honey's been bitten by the baby bug. At least one of my brothers isn't in the baby business." He looked at Dylan. "Are you?"

Dylan laughed. "Are you kidding? Who would I be having a baby with?"

"Samantha. You two are dating, aren't you?"

Were they? "I think so."

"Don't you know?"

"Sam's the cautious sort. It took me weeks to get her to admit the boyfriend she told me about was fictional. We're taking it slow."

"Meaning you haven't slept with her yet. Losing your touch, bro?"

"Fuck off," Dylan told him. "Sex isn't the only reason

I'm interested in a woman."

Sean started laughing. "You could've fooled me."

Dylan thought about pasting him one but decided it took too much effort. "It's not like that. I really like her."

"You always really like the women you date."

"This is different. She's—I'm—shit, I can't explain it." Not to himself, much less to anyone else.

"If I didn't know you I'd say you sounded serious."

Well, hell, maybe he was. "I think I could be."

"No shit?"

"You don't have to sound so happy about it."

Sean's shit-eating grin said it all. "About time you got tangled up over a woman. Wait until I tell Jack and Wyatt."

"There's nothing to tell." But he sure hoped there would be.

"Like hell there's not. I had twenty bucks on Sam finally breaking you down."

"You shitheads have a pool going?"

"Bet your ass we do. Dylan's finally taken the fall. The big L."

The big L? "I didn't say I was in love with her. Sweet Jesus, Sean, we haven't even—I can't be in love with her." Could he? "I said I *could* be serious. As in there's a possibility. That's a long way from being in love."

His brother was still grinning like the goddamn Cheshire cat. "Keep telling yourself that, bro."

Dylan's cell phone dinged, letting him know he had a

text. A good thing since he had no answer to Sean's bullshit. He pulled his phone out of his pocket and read the text, ignoring his brother.

Traced her to Concepción, Chile. Heading there now.

"It's from Hardeman about Glenna," he said and gave the phone to Sean.

Sean read it and grunted. "Chatty bastard, isn't he?"

Dylan gave a short laugh. "Yeah, I've yet to see an update from him that's longer than two lines."

"How in the hell has she managed to evade him for so long?"

Dylan shrugged. "Obviously, Glenna doesn't want to be found. Maybe this lead will pan out."

"Maybe, but I'm not holding my breath."

After Sean left, Dylan put Trouble back in his stall. He had other things he should be doing, but instead he saddled Hawkeye and went to check the fences. It gave him time to think and he always thought best on horseback.

Was Sean right? Was he in love with Sam?

How had he gone from wanting to get Sam into bed—which, of course, he still wanted—to being on the verge of falling crazy in love with her? Why Sam when he'd never been anywhere close to being in love before?

Before he met Sam he'd dated a number of women. Okay, make that a lot. He'd liked them, been fond of them, enjoyed them, admired them, lusted after them but he'd never been in love with any of them. He'd figured he never would be.

Maybe he was feeling this way because they hadn't had sex. Maybe then she wouldn't be a mystery, wouldn't be as fascinating. But he didn't think that was it.

Samantha was beautiful, but to be fair, he'd dated a lot of beautiful women. She was smart, but he'd always liked smart women. She was strong, sure of herself, extremely good at what she did. Which again, wasn't unusual among the women he'd been involved with.

But Sam had opened up to him. He wasn't sure why and he didn't know that she was either. When she'd told him about her past, she'd let him see a core of vulnerability that she kept well hidden from almost everyone else.

It made him feel like they had something special between them. Something he'd felt from the moment he met her.

Yeah, lust, you idiot.

Of course I have the hots for her. Who wouldn't? But that's not all it is.

Love? Damn, maybe I am in love with her.

"HOW'S IT GOING, Glory?" Dylan asked when he entered the kitchen. As usual, Glory was making something to eat. It looked like pie. Apple. His favorite.

"I'm good." She shot him a keen glance. "What do you want?"

"Who says I want anything? All I said was how's it going."

Glory pointed a floured finger at him. "I don't know why you boys think I'm a fool. I can read you like a book, just like I can every blessed one of you. Now, what is it you want?"

He shrugged and gave up. "Can you make something special for me to take to Sam's tonight? She doesn't want to leave the dog alone yet so I said I'd bring dinner." He added the clincher, since he knew Glory as well as she knew him. "If it's too much trouble I can just pick up a pizza or hamburgers."

"Oh, no you won't." She snorted. "Pizza or hamburgers, my foot. Anything special you want?"

"That chicken dish you make. The one we call Glory's special chicken. And that pie would be good too."

"I'll take care of it for you."

"You're the best," he told her and kissed her cheek.

"Don't you forget it," she told him with a laugh.

SAMANTHA STRIKER WAS a knockout. Tonight she wore jeans and a sweater and her hair was pulled back in a ponytail. She rocked that look. But hell, she even rocked scrubs. He itched to take the band out and bury his hands in the mass of blonde, silky hair. While he was kissing her. And while they were naked.

"Dylan? Did you hear what I said?"

"Sorry. I was thinking of something else." *Like getting you naked. Slow down, asshole,* he told himself. "What did you say?"

"I said dinner was delicious and asked if you'd thank Glory for me."

"Oh, sure. She'll be happy you liked it."

"What were you thinking about? You seemed so far away."

Nope, just as far as the bedroom. Or the couch. The table would work too. "I was thinking about you."

Having eaten dinner and cleaned up, they'd brought their wine glasses with them and were sitting on the couch in her living room. She looked at him quizzically and sipped her wine before setting it back on the coffee table. "What about me? Or should I ask?"

He grinned. "You can ask, but I'm not sure I should tell you."

She smiled back. "Never mind. I have a feeling I know."

She probably did.

Sam reached for his wine glass and set it beside hers on the table. Scooting closer to him, she laid her hand on his chest and said, "Ever since you kissed me last night—to be honest, before that too—I've thought about kissing you again."

"Feel free," he said, slipping an arm around her. "I promise I won't complain."

She put both arms around his neck and laid her lips on

his. No hesitation this time. Her tongue slipped into his mouth and he met it with his. His arms tightened around her and he pulled her closer. She came willingly.

Her lips were soft, so damn soft. She tasted sweet with a hint of fire. He deepened the kiss. Soon he was lying on his back, stretched out on the couch with Sam on top of him. He reached for the rubber band in her hair. "Can we get rid of this?"

She put her hand in her hair and pulled it out, shaking her head so her hair fell forward.

"God, your hair is so amazing." He sank his hands into it and brought her mouth to his. He kept one hand in her hair and moved the other down to slide over her ass and press her against him.

Sam groaned and pulled back to look at him. "Still cautious?" he asked her.

"Apparently not," she said, smiling. She sat up, straddling him with her legs on either side of his hips, reached for the hem of her sweater and pulled it off over her head, then tossed it aside. "I decided to take my chances."

"I'm glad." God, what an understatement. He filled his hands with her breasts, caressing her nipples through the fabric of her bra. She reached behind her to unhook her bra, thrusting her breasts forward. He pulled the straps down her arms and flung aside the bra, sucked in a breath at the sight of her naked breasts. "So beautiful," he said, cupping her breasts, running his hands over them, playing with her nipples, dusky pink and begging to be tasted. He guided one to his mouth, rolled it with his tongue, smiling at her gasp of pleasure.

Sam attacked his shirt buttons, spread the shirt open and put her hands on his chest. "You have such pretty muscles," she said. "It must be all the hard work you do."

He caressed her breasts and she wiggled around, sex against sex, until he was rock hard and aching to be inside her. She unbuttoned his jeans, got her hands on the zipper, but she was having a hard time getting them unzipped.

Shadow barked and she froze. "Ignore it," Dylan said, pulling her head down for a kiss. "He'll stop soon."

The noise was coming from her front hallway, which he assumed meant the dog had heard something at the front door or was looking out the window beside the door. Instead of calming down, Shadow's barking grew increasingly more agitated.

"Shit," he muttered under his breath.

"He's not stopping."

"No, he's not." He kissed her again and sighed.

"I'll go see what's wrong. Maybe someone's at the door, but it's pretty late for that." She got off the couch and bent down to pick up her sweater, not bothering with her bra. "Sorry," she said and put the sweater back on.

Yeah, sorry didn't even touch it.

He got up, buttoned and adjusted his jeans and followed her to the front hallway. Shadow was at the window, pawing at it, whimpering and barking almost hysterically. "What the hell is out there?"

"I have no idea," Sam said, flipping on the outside lights. She crouched down beside the dog, petting him and talking quietly to him. "It's okay, Shadow. Good dog. We've got it now." She looked out the window then back at him. "I can't see anything from here. Other than it's snowing like crazy."

"I don't see anything, either, but obviously Shadow does." Dylan opened the coat closet and pulled out his jacket. "I'll go out and look around."

"I'm going to stay here and hold Shadow. I don't think he'd run away if I let him go but I'm afraid he'll charge around and injure his leg again. He's awfully agitated. I wonder if it's a cat. Maybe he's one of those dogs who don't like cats." She grasped his collar firmly and opened the door.

That was possible, he supposed, but it was going to be an incredible pain in the ass if the dog freaked out every time he saw a cat. Especially when he came out to Dylan's, which he assumed he would. Dylan's cats were barn cats, although sometimes he'd find one that was clearly an inside cat and he'd keep it until he found it a home.

Dylan walked out and looked around. The snow was coming down heavily now. The street was quiet. He didn't see a soul outside besides himself. Not even a cat.

"Do you see anything?" Sam called out.

"Not yet." The exterior of the house looked fine, so he looked in the driveway where both his truck and Sam's car were parked. Briefly, he wondered why Sam hadn't parked in her garage. "I'll be damned. I found the problem," he called out to Sam, who was standing in the open doorway holding Shadow. "Your tires have been slashed. All four of them."

Chapter Eleven

*G*ODDAMN DOG. HOW *had it known he was outside the house? Maybe it just liked to bark. The porch light came on and she opened the door. He saw her holding the dog by the collar and the stupid dog barking like a maniac.*

Great. The boss was coming out to check on things. Having seen Dylan's truck, he'd known the boss was there but he'd figured the two of them would be too busy screwing each other to pay attention to anything else.

He hadn't counted on the goddamn dog going apeshit crazy and bringing them both out. At least the bitch was holding back the dog. He didn't doubt the animal would head straight for him.

Just before he faded away, he heard Dylan say, "I'll be damned. I found the problem. Your tires have been slashed. All four of them."

Smiling, he hopped a fence and began walking the two blocks to get to his truck. Yes, indeed. Everything was going according to plan.

THAT'LL TEACH ME to park in the driveway, Sam thought.

Dylan insisted they call the police and report the crime. Sam didn't argue, since having her tires slashed—in her driveway—was pretty disturbing. The gas tank was one thing. After all, they couldn't prove anything about that, no matter how suspicious they were about what had really taken place. But someone slashing her tires was a deliberate and vindictive action. Was someone trying to send her a message? And if so, who?

She called the police, saying she needed to report a crime. Then she was put on hold so she waited. And waited. And waited until finally someone came to the phone. She explained what had happened and was told it could be hours before someone could check it out and briefly explained why.

"No, I understand. Yes, we'll wait," she said, ending the call. "They're not sure when they can send someone," she told Dylan. "There was a wreck just outside of town that's got traffic piled up and all the police who can be spared are out there. I'm going to check in with the hospital and make sure they don't need me."

"Do you need to go in?" Dylan asked when she got off the phone with the hospital. "I can take you in my truck. Your car won't be going anywhere but Dillon's garage."

"No, they said most of the injuries are minor and they can take care of the couple that aren't."

"I guess we wait, then. I'll go take some more pictures. I snapped some when I went out the first time."

"Pictures of what?"

"Footprints. What's left of them, anyway. It's snowing pretty heavily. By the time the cops get here they'll be completely gone."

"I would never have thought to do that."

"Crime shows and books on crime. I have no idea if pictures taken with my cell phone will actually be useful but I figure it can't hurt."

They turned on an old movie while they waited. Dylan wrapped his arm around her and she snuggled against him. *I'll just close my eyes for a little bit*, Sam thought.

The next thing she knew she woke up to Dylan getting up from the couch. "I'm going to take Shadow out. He's been whining for a while now."

Sam rubbed her eyes and looked at the clock on the DVR. "Oh, well. I guess they're not coming."

Just then her doorbell rang. Sam looked out the window, saw a cop standing there and opened the door. A pleasant young woman, probably a few years younger than Sam said, "Dr. Striker? I'm Officer May Rogers. I'm sorry it took us so long to get here."

"That's all right. Did you get the accident cleared?"

"Yes, thanks. I understand someone slashed your tires?"

"That's right. Come in, Officer."

"If you don't mind, I'll look around outside first."

"May, is that you?" Dylan asked, coming in with Shadow still on the leash.

"Dylan? I thought that was your truck. Were you here when the incident occurred?"

"We both were. Shadow here sounded the alert." He motioned to the excited dog at his side, who clearly wanted to meet the new person.

May stepped forward and held out the back of her hand to Shadow. He sniffed her and licked her hand, apparently approving. "How long ago was this?" May asked.

"About two hours ago. Maybe a little less," Dylan said.

"All right. I'll check it out and then I'll be back to take your statements."

Sam shut the door and then said to Dylan, "Is there anyone in Marietta you haven't dated?"

"How do you know I dated May?"

She rolled her eyes. "Didn't you?"

"Well, yeah, but it was a long time ago."

Sam sighed, shook her head and started to go to the living room but Dylan stopped her with a hand on her arm.

"Does it bother you?"

She didn't ask what. She knew. "Honestly? I'm not sure."

He let go of the dog's leash and put his hands on both her arms, looking down at her. "It shouldn't."

She stared at him, thinking what pretty eyes he had. "Why?"

"None of them were you," he said, and kissed her.

"That sounds very romantic," she said a few minutes later.

"And you're not buying it."

"Let's just say I'm a little skeptical."

"I'll have to think of a way to convince you that I'm telling you the truth."

"I'M AFRAID WE won't have much luck finding who did this," May said, after taking their statements. "There's no way to get footprints since it's been snowing so hard. There's a high likelihood that some neighborhood kids are responsible."

"Aren't they more likely to toilet paper the house?" Sam asked.

"Depends on their age."

"Before I forget," Dylan said, "I took some pictures of the footprints earlier. I don't know whether they'll be useful to you or how good they are."

"Good thinking. Watch a lot of mysteries, do you?" May asked him with a twinkle in her eyes.

He smiled and handed her his phone. "Crime shows and police dramas. *CSI* and things like that."

May flipped through the digital photos. "Can you email these to me? We'll see what we can do with them."

"There's something else," Sam said. She and Dylan had decided that the mystery of her gas disappearing should be mentioned, in case it was related. Sam didn't know whether to think it was or not, but it was a strange coincidence at the very least. "Yesterday someone drained my gas tank. At least, that's what we think happened." Sam went on to tell her the circumstances.

May took notes in the small notebook she'd pulled from her pocket. Some cops used tablets now, particularly in the larger cities, but it seemed May liked the old-fashioned way of taking notes. "Are you sure it was drained?" she asked Sam, but immediately looked at Dylan, which annoyed Sam.

Sam shot Dylan a glance and shrugged. He said, "We're not positive but Sam is fairly certain she had at least a quarter of a tank earlier that day."

May had clearly wanted to put it down to kids making trouble but with the additional circumstances she looked more thoughtful. "That does put a bit of a different spin on it, assuming that's what happened."

"I can't think of anyone who would do something like this," Sam said.

"No fights with your neighbors? Or kids in the neighborhood?"

"No, nothing like that."

"We'll see what we can find out," May said as she stood. "Good to see you, Dylan. I'll be in touch."

I bet you will, Sam thought. *With Dylan.* She shook off that thought. She had no reason to think May Rogers was anything other than a good cop. *You're jealous, that's the problem. You're going to have a hard time if you get jealous of every woman Dylan's ever dated.*

Women Dylan dated. Could that be it?

"Are you going to be all right here?" Dylan asked Sam. "I don't think they'll be back, not tonight anyway. But if you're worried I can stay or you can bring Shadow and come home with me."

"I'm not worried. I'll be fine. Apparently, I have a guard dog." She gave Shadow, curled up on his pillow and snoring, an affectionate glance.

Dylan frowned. "I don't like leaving you. Let me stay. I'll sleep on the couch."

"You're sweet, but—"

"Are you sure you can't think of anyone who has a beef with you?"

"Not in Marietta. And I can't see anyone from Texas following me here. Why would they?"

"I guess it depends on how many people you pissed off when you volunteered at the shelter. Or maybe it's someone you operated on who had a bad outcome."

"There's another possibility we haven't discussed."

"What's that?"

"What if it's one of your ex-girlfriends? There are bound to be a few who weren't happy when you two broke up."

He laughed. "So, she's what? Harassing you? What point would there be to that?"

"Maybe she wants you back and thinks if you're not with me you'll give her another chance. Who was your last girlfriend?"

"It sure as shit wasn't her. Rebecca's gotten engaged to someone since we quit dating." He shook his head. "No, I can't see it. She'd have to be crazy or obsessed and I never dated anyone like that."

"It's at least as likely as someone from my past following me here. But if you ask me, neither sounds very likely. I'm sure the two things are unrelated. Like the officer said, tonight was probably just bored kids."

"Maybe. But you still need to be careful."

"I will. Now you need to go home. I'm sure you have to get up before dawn." She walked him to the front door. As he was putting on his coat, she said, "I'm sorry about earlier."

Dylan smiled and pulled her to him. "Me too. But there'll be other times." His mouth came down on hers, hard and hungry, leaving her in no doubt as to his plans for those 'other times'.

By the time he released her she was tingling all over.

"Count on it," he told her and left.

She watched him walk to his truck. *Resistance is futile.* Whoever said that had summed up her situation perfectly.

Chapter Twelve

DYLAN DIDN'T SEE Sam for the next few days. Some things came up at the ranch that he needed to take care of and she went back to work, so they weren't able to get together. But he talked to her each night, making sure nothing else out of the ordinary had happened and checking on how Shadow was doing. And wishing he was with her.

Damn it, Sean was right. He'd fallen in love with Sam. No matter what he told himself—he hadn't known her that long, there was still a lot he didn't know about her, she was no different from any other woman he'd been with, and a big one, he hadn't even made love to her yet—it didn't matter. He'd fallen for her. The fact that with Sam he thought of it as making love, not having sex or any of the myriad other ways to phrase the act, was telling in itself. No matter what, he kept coming back to the fact that he didn't just enjoy Sam or want to get her into bed. No, he was head over bootheels in love with Samantha Striker.

And he was almost a hundred percent sure that Sam was not in love with him. Yet.

A few days later, Sam came out to the ranch one afternoon to meet all of the horses. She brought Shadow with her, but since he'd recently been neutered, she left him in the kitchen with Glory to make sure he didn't overdo it.

They went out the kitchen door to go to the stables and then on to the pasture where most of the horses stayed during daylight. Occasionally one stayed in for various reasons, but Dylan was a believer in pasturing his horses as much as he could. "Hold on a minute," Dylan said. He tugged her to him, leaned down and kissed her. "Hi," he said, still holding her close.

"Hi." She smiled up at him and he thought again how pretty she was.

"I'm not sure how you do it, but you get prettier every time I see you."

Sam laughed. "I doubt that but thanks."

He kissed the tip of her nose. "Never doubt it. Let's take you to meet my horses."

They walked down to the stables and Dylan showed her around. He'd been out mending fences all morning and hadn't been anywhere but the tack room since he came in. But now he noticed that more than one of the stalls hadn't been mucked out. Dammit, that was supposed to be Jim's job but he was nowhere to be seen. Failing Jim, one of the other hands usually handled that chore. "Hold on a minute," he said to Sam and yelled for Jim. "Shit," he said when Jim never showed up. "This guy is never where he's supposed to be, when he's supposed to be there. I haven't seen him since before lunch."

"I saw someone a little earlier when I drove up. Dark hair, clean-shaven. Medium height, maybe. That's the impression I got, anyway. Could that be him?"

"Might be, although there are others around here you could describe that way. Was he young or old?"

"Maybe in his thirties. It was hard to tell because I only saw him for a minute and at a distance. It was a little odd. I could have sworn he was staring right at me but then he disappeared when I got out of the car."

"Sounds like him. Connor's been around him the most and he thinks he's weird. All I know is if he doesn't start doing his job better I'll have to fire him. And finding anyone to take his place at this time of year won't be easy."

He took her out to the pasture and told her a little about each horse. She was very complimentary of his horses, sincerely so, he thought. Sam was good about not bullshitting people. He'd found that out when Clay got injured.

"Are you too cold or do you want to see Trouble? He's out in the round pen. I worked with him some before you got here."

"Of course I want to see your new stallion. It's not nearly as cold today as it was the day we found Shadow."

"True." He looked up at the blue sky. Not a cloud in it and the sun was warming everything up.

They went out to the round pen. "What do you think?"

Dylan asked Sam. Trouble was on the other side of the pen. The stallion had been a real pain in the ass earlier when he was working with him. But that was nothing new.

"He's beautiful, Dylan. He looks like a buckskin."

"He's a brown dun. *Brunblakk* in Norwegian."

"His mane is gorgeous, but it looks like it's never been cut. Sunshine has a clipped mane. So does Riptide. I thought that was more common with this breed."

"It is. All of my other Norwegian Fjords are clipped. But Trouble doesn't like people messing with him. We damn near had to sedate him for the vet to examine him."

"I think it's gorgeous the way it is. I'm not sure I'd cut it. What's his story? I know you mentioned he was abused. Do you know anything about that?"

"Not a lot. His previous owner could never get him to settle down. According to him, the person who had him before him is the reason he's so touchy. Claims he wasn't the one who scarred him."

"You don't sound too sure of that."

Dylan rolled a shoulder. "All I know is someone abused him. He's got scars on his legs and his rump that don't look accidental." He sighed. "I'd really like to breed him but the jury's still out on that. I've been trying to get him used to the other horses so I can pasture them together. I think he'd do better if he had some company."

"He's been watching us the whole time we've been here."

"Probably trying to decide where he's going to kick me

next."

"He looks sweet."

Dylan laughed. "Sweet? Anything but."

She whistled and Trouble lifted his head. She whistled again. "Trouble, come see me, boy."

"You have to bribe him to get him close enough to put the line on him. He won't come without—"

Damned if the horse didn't start ambling over. He still appeared suspicious but Dylan had the feeling that was for his benefit and not Sam's. He was sure of it when Trouble went right up to her.

"Aren't you pretty?" Sam crooned, laughing when he put his nose in her chest and pushed. She rubbed his nose and spoke quietly to him.

"Careful, he bites." But he had to admit, Trouble was acting like a different horse.

"I don't think he wants to bite me," she said.

Sam kept patting him, talking so quietly to the horse that Dylan only heard snatches. He hoped she was right and Trouble wouldn't change his mind. But hell, he thought, watching the two of them, the stallion was all but purring.

"I'm having a hard time believing he's as bad as you've told me. He's a sweetheart."

That sure as shit wasn't how Dylan would have described him. "Watch him when he's with anyone but you. As far as I know, he's never acted this way with anyone else. Any other human, at any rate. You seem to have the magic touch."

"Do you have anything to give him? A sugar cube or a carrot?"

Dylan fished in his pocket for one of the sugar cubes he usually kept there. Handing it to her he said, "How would you feel about working with Trouble? I could use some help with him."

She laughed while feeding him the sugar. "Right. I'll fit it in between shifts."

"I'm serious. You're the first person he's ever warmed up to. He doesn't even like Burt. Well, he tolerates him but he's not crazy about him."

"Burt? One of your dogs, right?"

"Yes. See that big fuzzy guy over there?" He gestured to the big dog lying in the sun by the barn. "All horses like Burt. Except Trouble."

"Why do you think I could do anything with him when your brother Sean couldn't? Isn't he supposed to have the magic touch with horses?"

"Because Trouble didn't take to him like he has you. Look at him. He's crazy about you."

"Dylan, I'm a doctor, not a horse whisperer."

He laughed.

"What's so funny?"

"That's exactly what Sean used to say."

"STAY FOR DINNER," Dylan said to Sam when they finished

EVE GADDY

cooling down Trouble and getting him set for the evening. "Glory made beef stew."

"I should probably take Shadow home. I haven't fed him."

"Sam." She looked at him. "I have dog food."

Of course he did. There went that excuse. And really, why was she hesitating?

"Are you worried I'll ask you to stay?"

"Not worried, exactly."

He smiled and pulled her into his arms. "Stay," he said, stringing kisses along her jawline. "For dinner. And tonight." He kissed her mouth, a long, slow, drugging exchange of lips and tongues. He went to work on her neck.

"I can't think when you do that." But, God, it felt so good.

"Why do you need to think?" He kissed her mouth again. If he kept this up they'd be naked and making love in no time.

There was no doubt they wanted each other. She felt him against her, already hard. Was she making a mistake? Again? She didn't believe Dylan would hurt her like the men in her last three disastrous relationships had. But neither was she certain she could sleep with Dylan and not become more involved with him than he was with her. Oh, he'd said they were involved, that he, at least, was involved, but his reputation still made her uneasy.

Or was he ready to stop playing the field and be with one

woman? Her. Perhaps not forever, because God knew, she wasn't sure she was ready for that. But she wanted more than sex just for the fun of it.

He held her close, nuzzling aside her coat to get to her collarbone. She was melting. She closed her eyes, felt his lips on her neck once more, and thought about the night at her house, before Shadow alerted them that something was wrong. Oh, yes, Dylan would definitely be fun. She hadn't worried about anything that night. She'd gone with the flow. If her tires hadn't been slashed she wouldn't be having this stupid, irritating conversation with herself.

He stopped kissing her, but still held her close. Sam opened her eyes and stared at him. At his mouth, his lips firm, but soft. And oh, so talented.

"I see the wheels turning. Is this really that difficult of a decision?"

His eyes had darkened to jade. He was a beautiful man. She wanted to put her hands on his bare chest, feel his hands on her. Feel his hands everywhere. On her bare skin instead of through her heavy coat. So why the hesitation?

"Hell," she said, and laid her lips on his. That's all it took. He backed her into the tack room, closed the door and pushed her up against it. How could kissing him, only kissing him, make her feel like melting? Sam shoved him back and stripped off her coat. When he saw what she was doing, he did the same. And then she was in his arms again, backed against the door, her legs around his hips and Dylan hard against her. She wanted her jeans gone. She wanted his gone. But he was kissing her, and she was drowning.

He let her down slowly. Undid her buttons, one by one, his expression fierce. When he finished, he pushed her shirtsleeves down her arms and let the shirt flutter to the floor. Her bra came next. He unhooked it, stripped it off of her and flung it aside. Her nipples pebbled, both from his intense scrutiny and from the chill in the air. He cupped her breasts, then lowered his head and licked her nipple, then drew it slowly into his mouth and sucked on it.

"Take your shirt off," she said when he would have switched to her other breast.

Damn, he had a great smile. She wanted to rip off both their clothes right now.

"Whatever you want." He unbuttoned the top few buttons and then pulled off the shirt over his head. She had a brief moment to admire the white T-shirt that covered his broad chest and muscular arms and then he yanked it off too.

He picked her up and she wrapped her legs around his hips again. She kissed him, rubbed her bare breasts against his skin. They both groaned.

"Are you on the pill? Or something else?" he asked hoarsely.

"Yes. But…"

Chapter Thirteen

DYLAN KNEW WHY Sam hesitated. She was cautious. Careful. Who would have thought her reaction would make him hotter? He had a rule. Never have sex without a rubber. He'd almost broken that rule with Sam. That bothered him. Briefly. Why Sam?

Because you're in love with her, dumbass.

"Dylan?"

He let her down, groaning as her breasts rubbed against his chest. Stepping back, he bent to pick up her sweater and handed it to her. "Let's go to the house." He found his flannel shirt and put it on. Sam was still holding her sweater, looking around.

"Do you see my bra?"

"No, but you don't need it. I'm going to take off that sweater again in about five minutes."

"What about Glory?"

"Glory?"

"Yes, Glory, your housekeeper. We can't go to the house and immediately disappear. What would she think?"

Dylan had his coat on and helped Sam into hers. He zipped it up, spied her bra and gave it to her to stuff in her pocket. "She'd think we were going to do exactly what we *are* going to do." He kissed her briefly. "But she's gone home by now so don't worry about it."

He grabbed her hand and left the tack room, intent on getting her to the house as quickly as humanly possible.

Sam was laughing as he pulled her along. "Can you slow down so I can keep up without running?"

"No." He heard Connor calling him. Cursing him under his breath, he halted, turned around and gritted out, "What?"

"I won't be here tomorrow, Boss. Remember, I have a dentist appointment."

"Fine." He turned his back and started walking again. Sam was biting her lip to keep from laughing. All it did was make him want some of that himself.

"Jim should be here," Connor continued. "Least he said he would. He took off early today."

Dylan halted again and looked back at Connor, who was grinning, knowing full well, he'd wager, what Dylan was up to. Or trying to be up to. "Connor?"

"Yeah, Boss?"

"I really don't give a shit."

Dylan couldn't tell who laughed harder, Connor or Sam.

Five minutes later they were in his room, ripping off each other's clothes. He'd forgotten about Shadow, who he'd left outside the door barking indignantly. He swore, stopped kissing Sam long enough to let the dog in, then pulled her into his arms again, ignoring the disapproving look from the dog. "Get used to it," he told him, causing Sam to laugh.

When he got down to his jeans he went to the bathroom to find what was left of the last box of condoms he'd had. He wasn't sure where he'd left them, or even, unfortunately, if he actually had any since he hadn't needed one for several months now.

"Dylan? What are you doing?"

She was waiting for him. Naked. In his bed. And he couldn't find the goddamn condoms. There were a couple of places in his bedroom where they might be. He went back in the bedroom and sure enough, she was lying on his bed. But she wasn't naked. She wore a tiny pair of panties and nothing else.

"Damn, you're beautiful."

She smiled. "Thank you. But why am I all alone here? What are you doing, Dylan?" Her voice was low and husky. And very, very tempting.

"Looking for a condom." He pulled out the top drawer in his dresser and halle-freakin'-lujah, there they were. He crossed the room, tossed the box on the bedside table, unzipped his jeans and got rid of them, and then he was gathering Sam's nearly naked, curvy body against his. He kissed her, ran his hands over her sweet ass and that's all it took to make him hard again.

Sam slid her hand down, wrapped it around his cock and he thought he'd died and gone to heaven. Returning the favor, he slipped his hand inside her panties and his finger inside of her. They both moaned.

"Slower next time," he said, grabbing a condom. Sam took it from him, unwrapped it and rolled it down over his cock. He kissed his way down her stomach, stripped off those tiny panties and admired her for about five seconds before he spread her legs and drove inside her.

She was hot, wet and so damn tight. Her legs wrapped around him, her muscles gripped him, her hips bucked as she met each thrust, pulling him deeper inside her with every movement. Each time he drove inside her she tightened around him. He felt her orgasm rip through her, heard her cry out, and he came in a mind-blowing rush of pleasure.

After a while he realized he was crushing her and rolled off of her. He got up, got rid of the condom, then slipped back in bed with her. Wrapping her in his arms, he kissed her and said, "That was amazing."

Sam laughed softly. "Yes, it was."

Damn. He was crazy in love with Sam. There was no denying it any longer.

Fine, but you don't need to tell her. It's too soon. You've only now gotten her into bed. Do you want to push her away?

No. But I want her to know we have something special. At least for me.

What if she's not ready to hear it? What if she just wants to have fun? Like you usually do.

Oh, shut up.

"Dylan, is something wrong?"

"No, everything is right." He kissed her and added, "I was just having a little argument with myself."

"What about?"

"You and me."

"This isn't where you dump me, is it?"

He had to laugh. "No. Far from it."

"Oh, good. You had me worried for a minute there."

"You don't need to worry." *Don't do it, dumbass. It's too soon. Way too soon.*

"Are you going to let me in on what's going on or do you plan to argue with yourself all day?"

"I'm in love with you, Sam." Well, hell, there it was.

Her eyes widened and she stared at him. "What did you say?"

"I'm in love with you," he repeated. She didn't look like she believed him. He pulled her closer. Kissed her cheek, her jawline, the corner of her mouth. "I've never told a woman who wasn't family that I loved her."

Sam looked at him solemnly, her hand over his heart. "If you were anyone else and we were anywhere else, I'd think you told me that just to get me into bed. But since I'm already here I know that's not it."

"No. I'd be pretty pathetic if I had to tell a woman I loved her to get her into bed." He kissed her, long enough to make both of them want more. "I can't get you out of my head. I think about you every day. I dream about you every night. It's making me crazy."

"I don't know what to say to you."

"I suppose 'I love you too' is out of the question?"

She smiled. "How about I'm crazy about you, Dylan?"

"That'll work," he said.

Sam kissed him, pushed him onto his back and asked, "Where are those condoms?"

Dylan grinned. "You really are my kind of woman."

LATER, WHEN BOTH of them discovered they were starving, they went to the kitchen and raided the refrigerator. Dylan got out the stew Glory had made, ladled it into a couple of bowls and microwaved them. Glory had also left a loaf of French bread wrapped in foil with instructions to warm it up to go with the stew. He grinned, reading the note.

"What's so funny?" Sam asked.

"Glory thinks I'm totally helpless in the kitchen." He gave Sam the note and turned on the oven.

"Don't forget to preheat the oven for the bread. On bake, not broil! And don't unwrap it, either," Sam read aloud. "Not broil is all in caps. What did you do?"

"I was in a hurry one time—one lousy time—so I decided to heat up the loaf without the foil in the broiler."

"Oops."

"Oops is right. It didn't work too well. Especially when I

forgot and left it in there. I didn't realize the broiler would go up in flames."

Sam laughed. "What a mess."

"Yeah. I guess that's why she feels the need to leave me the same damn note every time."

"Poor thing," she said, and patted his cheek. "Be grateful she cooks for you."

"I am. Believe me, I am." He poured them both a glass of wine and took them to the table. Then once the bread was hot, he brought the rest.

Sam wore one of his T-shirts and, he was almost sure, nothing else. He was so distracted by trying to figure out the answer to that question, he almost forgot to eat.

"He really is appropriately named," Sam said, gesturing at Shadow who'd followed them to the kitchen.

"Pain in the ass would also be appropriate," Dylan said, reminded of when he'd stood outside the bedroom door and barked until he let him in.

"Don't you listen to him, Shadow. Can I help it if he loves me?" she asked, looking at Dylan.

"No. It's impossible not to."

"Flatterer."

"Nope. God's honest truth."

After they finished they went back to his room and he found the answer to what she wore underneath the T-shirt. Absolutely nothing.

"Damn it, who keeps calling me?" Dylan said much later,

when his cell phone buzzed yet again.

"Maybe you should answer it. If they've called this many times it could be important."

"Everyone who might be making an emergency call to me is on my list of favorites. Which means it would ring through instead of buzz."

"Still. You should see who it is."

"Shit. I've finally got you exactly where I want you. Naked, in my bed. Talking to anyone but you is the last thing on my list of what I want to do."

Sam laughed and propped herself up. She kissed him lightly and said, "I'm not going anywhere. Answer your phone."

He got up and walked over to the dresser where he'd left the phone. "Just like I thought," he said, looking at the list of callers. "I don't recognize the number. And they didn't leave a message. None of the five times they called."

His phone buzzed again while he was holding it so he answered. "This better be good. You've got ten seconds to tell me who this is and what the hell you want." The moment he said that it dawned on him that it could be Glenna calling him. Before he could ask the caller spoke.

"Dylan, thank God you picked up. It's Gretchen. Gretchen Hoffman."

Gretchen? He'd run into her a couple of months ago in town. She'd had a black eye, which she'd tried to hide with makeup but it hadn't worked. During the short time they'd talked, Gretchen had been looking over her shoulder for fear her husband would see her and, Dylan didn't doubt, lay into her again. Her husband was a class A controlling, wife-beating asshole. He'd forbidden Gretchen to talk to Dylan, never mind that they'd known each other since they were six and had gone to school together from then until they graduated high school. Dylan was sure he wasn't the only person her husband had forbidden her to see.

"What's wrong?"

"It's Frank. He—he—I've got to get out of here. Before he comes back."

He could tell she was fighting tears. "What did the bastard do to you?" This time, he thought, but didn't add.

"My face is…pretty bad. I think he broke some ribs too. And—oh, God, Dylan. I can't talk about it. He took my keys. He's down at the Wolf Den. He could be back any time and I'm afraid of what he'll do if I'm still here. He—he was drunk when he left. He'll be worse."

"Did you call the police?"

"No! I can't. The last time I called them he nearly killed me."

Maybe he could convince her to go to the police later. But for now he just needed to get her away, somewhere the fucker couldn't find her. "I'll come get you."

"Thank you. Dylan, I'm so sorry to drag you into this. I didn't know who else to call."

Because her shithead husband had alienated her from

most if not all of her friends and family. "You're at home, right? Can you get out of there? Go to a neighbor's until I can get there?"

"No. They're all afraid of him."

She didn't elaborate but she didn't need to. He could imagine what the bastard had done to make sure no one helped her. "I'll be there as soon as I can."

He hung up and rubbed his hands over his face. "Shit. Goddamn it." He looked at Sam who was sitting up with the sheet drawn up over her breasts. "I have to go help out a friend." But what the hell could he do with her once he picked her up? Take her to a woman's shelter? Where the hell was a shelter? What if she wouldn't go? He picked up his jeans and boxers and stepped into them, then looked around for a shirt. Where in the hell was the shirt he'd been wearing?

"I gathered that. Can I do anything to help?"

He started to lay it all out for her and then he remembered. The last thing Sam wanted or needed was to get involved in a case of domestic violence. The very thing she'd left Dallas to avoid.

"Thanks, but I can handle it. I don't know how long I'll be gone." He gave up looking for his shirt and went to his closet to get a fresh one. "I'm really sorry but—" He stopped short as he came out of the closet to see Sam putting on her clothes. "You don't have to leave."

"I'm coming with you."

"No. Sam, you don't have to do that."

She gave him a rueful smile. "Yes. I do."

Chapter Fourteen

S AM BROUGHT SHADOW downstairs and put him in the mudroom with food, water and blankets for his bed. He was clearly unhappy to be left behind, but he accepted it. Then she wrote a quick note for Glory in case they weren't back by the time she came to work.

Dylan tried his best to talk her out of going with him. But it was obvious he didn't really know what he was doing. "Have you done this before?" Sam asked him.

"What, helped out a friend? Of course."

"That's not what I meant and you know it. What are you going to do once you pick her up?"

"Take her someplace safe. A women's shelter."

"Do you know how to get in touch with one?"

"No, but I'll figure it out."

"She wouldn't call the cops. How do you know she'll go to a shelter?"

"I don't, goddamn it. I'll bring her here if she won't."

"For how long? She can't stay here indefinitely. What if her husband figures out where she is?"

EVE GADDY

"He won't. There's no reason he would."

"Oh, Dylan, you know that's not true. This is Marietta. Someone will figure it out and eventually he'll hear about it."

He glared at her. "Shit, Sam, what do you want me to do?"

"I want you to quit arguing and let me come with you. I can help her, Dylan."

"That's not the point. The point is what will it do to you? Do you think I've forgotten why you moved to Marietta in the first place?"

It's time you get over it. Think of all the women and children you helped and not the few cases that had a bad outcome.

Yes, but murder is a bit worse than a bad outcome.

Stop. Stop thinking that way.

She put her hand on his arm. "I need to do this. It's time I dealt with it instead of running away."

"Sam, no one, especially not me, would blame you for not wanting to get involved in this kind of situation again. Don't put yourself through it."

"It's not up for argument. I'm going." She put her coat on.

Admitting defeat, Dylan shrugged, put his coat on and went out the back door with Sam following.

Sam used the time in the car to call the hospital for a phone number for the women's shelter in Billings. She was able to talk to someone from the shelter and arrange to bring Dylan's friend to them.

"The shelter has room for her," Sam told Dylan after

hanging up.

Dylan snorted. "Now we just have to convince her that's her best option."

"Do you know how long this has been going on? Is this the first you've heard of it?"

"I'm not sure but I wouldn't be surprised if the son of a bitch has been hitting her since they married. That was four or five years ago. He managed to cut her off from her friends and family by the time they'd been married a year. I saw her in town a few months ago, but it was by chance. She looked like shit, too. Besides the black eye she looked totally beat down."

"Did you and Gretchen date?" *Of course they did, dummy.*

He shot her a speculative glance. "For about two weeks, in high school. We've known each other since we were six. We were always more friends than anything else."

What did it say about her that she found his response comforting?

Idiot. It says you've fallen for him.

Ten minutes later they pulled up to a small, wood-frame house on the outskirts of Marietta.

Gretchen Hoffman was probably a pretty woman when her eye wasn't swollen nearly shut and her mouth double its usual size with a split lip. She was small and slim with brown hair and brown eyes and she wasn't happy to see Dylan show up with a woman she didn't know. She hugged Dylan, then noticing Sam, asked, "Who is this? Why is she here?"

Dylan introduced them and Gretchen pulled him aside. Sam heard snatches of conversation, enough to know the woman was suspicious of her. But apparently Dylan got through to her.

"Dylan says you're a doctor."

"Yes, I'm a trauma surgeon. Would you let me examine you and see if you need to go to the hospital?"

"I don't. I just need to get away before he comes back. He'll calm down in a day or two."

"He'll calm down?" Dylan asked incredulously. "You're going back to him? Are you kidding me?"

"I don't have a choice. I have no money, no job, and no skills. And I'm pregnant. How am I supposed to support a baby without money?" As soon as she said the last word, she doubled over and cried out.

Sam helped her to a chair. "How long have you been having these pains?"

"Not...long."

"Gretchen, tell her the truth," Dylan said.

"A few hours. Since he...beat me."

She wasn't telling them everything. Sam said to Dylan, "Can you go get some blankets? We need to get her to the hospital, now. She could be having a miscarriage."

Once Dylan left the room Sam said, "Gretchen, did he rape you?"

Tears ran down her cheeks as she nodded. "And then he

beat me. Don't tell Dylan… It will just upset him more."

"I won't. But don't worry about Dylan. You need to think about yourself."

"YOU WERE GREAT tonight with Gretchen," Dylan said, hours later back at the ranch. "Thank you."

Sam gave Shadow a last pat before leaving him to his bed. He'd been overjoyed to see them, as if they'd been gone days instead of hours.

"I'm glad I was able to help." She hesitated at saying anything else because he looked so hopeful. But she knew she should warn him that the outcome might not be what either of them wanted. "Dylan, you know this isn't the end of it, don't you? Gretchen was very reluctant to get the police involved. Plus, I'm not at all sure she'll go to the shelter once she's out of the hospital. All we can do is encourage her and give her the opportunity. In the long run, no one but Gretchen has control over what she decides. She could still go back to him."

He unbuttoned his shirt and threw it in the general direction of an overstuffed chair that sat in the corner of the room. "Why in the hell would she do that? The bastard beat the shit out of her and made her lose her baby." He sat on the bed and yanked off his boots.

"It's hard to understand. There are so many factors involved. Incomprehensible as it seems, she could still go back to him. I doubt they'll keep him in jail long." After taking her statement at the hospital, the police had picked up Frank Hoffman on domestic violence and assault charges. "If he comes to see her before she goes to the shelter and promises he'll never do it again—" She spread her hands. "She might forgive him. Then it would be up to the police as to whether they'll prosecute."

Dylan went to his dresser, opened a drawer and pulled out a clean T-shirt, which he handed to her. "Not that I mind you being naked, but I thought you might want something to sleep in."

"Thanks." Sam started undressing.

He sat on the bed and watched her. "Does that happen a lot? Once she gets away a woman goes back to the man who abused her?"

Sam pulled the T-shirt over her head. "It happens. More often than you'd think."

"How do you deal with it? I mean, you do all you can to help and then they go back and it's for nothing."

"The way I usually dealt with it was to give them my card with the shelter's number on it and tell them to call if they needed us. And then I helped someone else I hoped would get away and stay away." *And not get murdered. Don't forget that one.*

"You're thinking about Dallas." It wasn't a question. "Come here." Dylan pulled her between his legs and looked at her ruefully. "I'm sorry. I knew you shouldn't have come.

It was too big of a reminder."

She put her arms around him and pressed his head against her chest. "I'm glad I did. I needed to do it. I hope Gretchen sticks to her resolve, but even if she doesn't it felt good to be helping someone again."

He pulled back to look at her. "You're a doctor, for God's sake. You help people all the time."

"Yes, but not in the same way. The best thing is, I proved to myself that I can still do it. I might even be able to volunteer at a shelter again."

"Are you sure you want to?"

"I don't know. But at least it's a possibility now and it wasn't before. Let's go to bed. I'm exhausted and even though I don't go in until noon, I do have to work tomorrow."

He looked at the clock on the dresser. "It's going to be a short night."

Sam slept the remainder of the night in Dylan's arms. And thank God, she didn't dream.

Chapter Fifteen

SAM LEFT AROUND ten to take Shadow home and get ready for work. Dylan had been up for hours, taking care of his horses and doing whatever chores she imagined he had every morning.

"How can you look so wide awake?" she asked him before she left. "You couldn't have had more than three hours of sleep."

"Good genes," he said.

He kissed her, slow and leisurely, as if they had all day. It made her wish they did. "Will I see you tonight?" he asked her.

"No," she said regretfully. "I won't get off until ten. Later if I'm in the middle of an operation."

"Tomorrow night, then?"

"I can do that."

"Good, I'll see you tomorrow."

Sam drove home in a bit of a daze. Partly because of lack of sleep, but also because she was remembering the night before. Specifically, when Dylan had told her he loved her.

She believed him. Or rather, she believed that he *thought* he was in love with her. Whether he really was or not…that would take time to know for certain. She glanced at Shadow, sitting up in the passenger seat next to her and looking out the window, his tongue hanging out and panting happily. "What should I do, Shadow?"

Head tilted, Shadow looked at her and barked.

"Yes, I know you adore him. But since he's the one who found you and saved you, that's not a surprise."

Whatever she'd thought Dylan was going to say, *I'm in love with you* had been the last thing on her radar. And then he'd said it and he'd looked so sincere. She'd admitted she was crazy about him. But love? Love was complicated. Falling in love hurt. Whereas, if she wasn't in love with Dylan… Oh, shit. What did it matter what you called it? If they broke up it would still hurt just as badly.

Since she was leaving again in a little over an hour, she parked in her driveway. There was a note on her front door, held on by something that stuck out. As she drew closer she realized with a burst of nausea that a knife held the note pinned to her door.

Shadow growled as he nosed around, then whimpered while he tried to pull her away. "It's okay, Shadow." But it wasn't. It was sick.

Sam barely stopped herself from yanking on the knife and pulling it and the note off her door. Not that it would have fingerprints, but there was no sense making the cops' job harder for them. She stepped closer to read the letters cut out from magazines and newspapers.

You might have left Big D but you can't run from what you've done.

With shaking hands, she called the police. She asked for Officer Rogers and surprisingly got her. Sam told her what had happened, including that she hadn't been home since yesterday afternoon, which didn't narrow the time down by a whole lot. The officer promised to come right out.

She took Shadow around back, noticing thankfully that nothing seemed out of place. Unlocking and opening the door, she walked in holding her breath. Shadow wasn't flipping out, and she thought that was a good sign that whoever had left the note on the door hadn't been inside the house.

Sitting down at the kitchen table, she called the doctor who was working before her. Without giving any details, she asked if he could cover for her until she was able to get there, telling him it could be a while. "Thank you so much. I owe you," she said when he agreed.

Sam debated calling Dylan but decided to wait until she'd talked to Officer Rogers. Maybe she'd know something more by then.

HE WOULD HAVE *given his left nut to see how she'd reacted*

when she saw his little love note. He hoped the bitch was worried now. He had another note for her that he planned to put on her car windshield. Maybe tonight. He knew she was going to the hospital. It might be easier to do it there instead of at her house. What if she parked in her garage for a change?

She would pay for fucking with his marriage. For helping Sandy—his goddamn wife—leave him. And even more for testifying to a bunch of lies about him. Lies that had sent him to jail.

He'd had a right to slap Sandy around a little. Clumsy bitch. It was her fault she'd broken a rib or two. And that bitch doctor had manufactured the punctured lung. So what if she had a couple of black eyes? Besides, she'd deserved what she got. But Dr. Striker's testimony had made it sound much worse than it was.

A year in jail had been long enough for Sandy to manage to get lost permanently.

Lucky for him, and a bitch for her, the good doctor hadn't been so hard to trace.

TRUE TO HER word, Officer Rogers showed up not long after Sam reported the incident. She told Sam she wanted to examine the exterior of the house and the front door first, as well as take pictures. After she did that she came inside with the knife and note in separate plastic bags.

"Someone is coming out to dust for prints, but I'm not sure when they'll be here. One of our other officers usually does that, as we don't have a lot of crime here in Marietta."

"I have to go to work. Will that be a problem?" Sam looked at Shadow, who had gone to the officer when she came in and was now sitting with his head in her lap, occasionally nudging her to pet him. In spite of the circumstances she had to hide a smile. It was clear the officer was comfortable with dogs and liked them. Shadow was, apparently, in love.

"It shouldn't be. Since it doesn't appear anyone was inside, they can just dust the front door. Unfortunately, it's unlikely the suspect left any fingerprints."

No surprise there. "I'm worried about leaving Shadow here with the doggie door open. What if the intruder comes back and Shadow's outside? He might try to hurt Shadow, especially since Shadow would probably be barking his head off."

"It might be safer to keep him inside. Will you be gone for long?"

"Until about ten. Oh, well, the kitchen floor is tile anyway," Sam said, resigned.

Officer Rogers laughed. "We'll try to have someone do a drive by on the house a couple of times."

"That would be great. Thank you."

"Do you recognize the knife, Dr. Striker?"

Sam took the plastic bag from her and looked at the knife. "No, but it's a big sucker, isn't it? And please, call me Sam."

"All right, Sam. Call me May. Do you know what the note refers to?"

"I can't say for sure, but I volunteered at a women's shelter in Dallas. The Big D," she added in case May didn't know the nickname, although she probably did. "It might refer to one of those cases."

"You don't think it has anything to do with one of your operations? A bad outcome or something like that? In Dallas, since he mentions that specifically."

"I don't think so. I can't say absolutely not, of course." She sighed. "I had a really bad situation occur not long before I moved to Marietta." Sam told her about the murder, though not in as great a detail as she'd told Dylan.

"That's certainly something to look into," May said, making more notes.

"There's just one problem. The murderer is in jail."

May looked up from her notes. "Are you certain of that?"

"God, I hope he is. He's supposed to be. But since all this has happened, I've been wondering." She hadn't tried to find out, though. Probably because the thought of that murderer running free scared the shit out of her.

"I'll check into it and let you know. Is there any other incident you can think of that might help us identify this person? If this Baxter is still in jail then it follows that it was someone else in Dallas."

"I don't know. I'm sure I pissed off a lot of men when I helped the women at the shelter. I volunteered at the shelter for several years. But only a few of the men I testified against knew who I was. There were just a handful of cases where I had to actually appear in court."

"Can you make a list of them? You can email it to me."

"Okay, but it might be a while depending on how busy I am at work."

"No problem. It's going to take me a while to check on what I already have here."

Sam walked her to the door, with Shadow tagging along. "Thank you so much, and thanks for getting here so quickly."

"I'm glad I could." She hesitated a moment, then said, "If these incidents are tied together, which I believe they are, that means he's escalating in intensity. The knife and the note were definitely threatening. Be careful. Especially at home, but at work and wherever else you go too."

"Meaning Dylan's."

"Meaning anywhere. The suspect could be anywhere in Marietta, or possibly a nearby town. I'm going to see if I can get pictures of the men whose names you send me and see if you recognize anyone."

"May, you don't think this could be a woman, do you?"

"Well, it's possible," she said slowly. "But the knife and the note indicate a male more than a female. Do you know of any women who might have it in for you?"

"Only Dylan's ex-girlfriends," she said wryly. Realizing who she was talking to she flushed and added, "I didn't mean you."

May laughed. "Don' worry, I have a thick hide. Dylan and I grew up together. I'm not really one of his exes. We went out when we were in high school, and that's been awhile. Unless he's changed a lot, though, Dylan doesn't have jealous exes."

"That's what everyone tells me." And she believed it, mostly.

"The specific reference to Dallas—especially calling it Big D—makes it more likely, in my opinion, to be someone from your past, and not Dylan's."

"I think you're right. At first I wondered but this last thing convinced me it's someone out to get me specifically and not someone tied to Dylan."

She bent down to pet the dog. "Yes, Shadow, you're a good boy." To Sam she said, "He's awfully sweet. How long have you had him?"

"Not long. Dylan found him and gave him to me."

She laughed. "That's Dylan. There's not a stray in Marietta, or to be honest, the state of Montana that he wouldn't pick up and try to help."

Sam laughed too. "It didn't take long for me to figure that out. The sheer number of dogs he has at his ranch was a pretty strong hint."

"I know, and Lord knows how many more he'd have if we didn't have an animal rescue place called Whiskers and Paw Pals."

"Really? I didn't know that."

"Yes. They take all kinds of animals, though. Dylan takes dogs and cats, but especially dogs. They seem to gravitate to him."

That was for sure.

"Take care," May said. "I'll be in touch."

Chapter Sixteen

SAM GOT HOME fairly late and by the time she'd taken Shadow out, fed him and checked the kitchen for accidents—surprisingly, he hadn't had one—it was closing in on eleven. She debated not calling Dylan but she knew he'd be upset if she didn't tell him about the knife and note until tomorrow. And she wanted to talk to him. There was something very comforting about Dylan. Now that she'd had time to really think about it, this latest incident had increased her concern to fear of what the perpetrator planned next.

It worried her a little that she relied on Dylan so easily when in the past she'd always been always been able to take care of herself. Not that talking to him meant she wasn't self-reliant. Still… *Oh, stop second-guessing yourself and call him.*

She punched in his number. He answered on the second ring. "Hi. I didn't expect to hear from you tonight. What's up?"

"Did I wake you? I know it's late but I took a chance you'd still be up."

"I was headed for bed but I haven't gotten there yet. What's wrong, Sam?"

"I had an incident here at my house earlier today. After I got back from the ranch."

"What kind of an incident?"

She took a breath and told him the whole story. When she finished there was utter silence. "Dylan?"

"I'm coming over."

"Don't be ridiculous. It's late and you get up at the crack of dawn."

"Why didn't you tell me about this when you found it?"

"First off, there was nothing you could do other than freak out." Which he was doing right now. "I called the cops and told May and by the time she finished here, I had to go to work. If I'd called you then you'd have wanted to come over. I didn't have time to argue."

"I wish you'd told me."

"I'm sorry. I thought it would be better to wait. I wasn't even at home all day, so you coming over would have been pointless."

"You shouldn't be alone. What if the crazy bastard comes back?"

"My doors are locked and May said she'd have the police drive by tonight a few times. Besides, I have Shadow."

"The dog is not a match for a crazy man with a knife. If you don't want me to come over, why don't you and Shadow come here?"

"Because it's late, I'm exhausted and nothing's going to happen."

"You should have a burglar alarm."

"In Marietta? Nobody has a burglar alarm here. Well, maybe the stores but I bet there aren't ten people in town who have an alarm."

"I don't like it. You shouldn't be alone. Damn it, this is just getting worse. What's he going to do next?"

"You're sweet to worry, but you're making me wish I hadn't told you until tomorrow."

"Goddamn it, Sam. This can't be explained away as a prank any longer."

"I'm aware of that, Dylan."

"I know you are; I'm just worried about you."

She sighed. "Would it make you feel better to know I have a gun?"

"Absolutely. Do you?"

"Yes." She hadn't kept it loaded, though, since she'd moved to Marietta. It hadn't seemed a necessity in the small town. Marietta had very little crime. "I know how to use it. But I seriously doubt I'll need it." She hoped to God she wouldn't. Given her work at the women's shelter in Dallas, and the not-so-safe parts of town she'd had to visit, she'd gotten her concealed carry license. But growing up on a ranch in Texas, she'd always had guns and knew how to shoot. She'd never had to shoot a person, and she hoped like hell she never would. Rattlesnakes, yes. People, no.

"Better to have it and not need it than need it and not have it," Dylan said.

Changing the subject slightly, she said, "May is looking into where Baxter is. If he's still in jail. She's also looking into a list of names I gave her of other men I testified against, or who knew I worked at the shelter. But if Baxter is out of prison, he's the most likely suspect."

"He's out of jail after being convicted of murder? I know that it happens, but that's insane."

"I don't know that he is. But he could be."

"When will you know?"

"Tomorrow, possibly. May said she'd call me as soon as she knows. By the way, I really like her."

"She's a good person. And a good cop. She'll work hard to find out who's responsible. But in the meantime, are you sure you don't want to come out here tonight? Or let me come there?"

"Dylan, I'm fine. Honestly."

"You are right now. And I want to make sure you stay that way."

"I'll sleep with my gun beside me. With that and Shadow to warn me if he hears something, not to mention the cops driving by, I'll be safe."

"Damn, you're stubborn."

"I know. And you worry too much."

After making plans to go to the ranch the following day, Sam hung up. Then she went to her closet, got her handgun out of the locked box, loaded it and put it in her bedside table drawer.

SAM SPENT THE following day at the ranch. Shadow was well enough that she could let him out on his own, though she still kept an eye on him and called him to her side if she thought the dogs were getting too rowdy.

She worked with Trouble and thought she was making progress with him. Sam was no horse whisperer, but even she had to admit that she and the horse had a special bond. Trouble would now come when she called him, and often followed her around like a dog. Today she'd put a saddle blanket on his back to see what he thought.

She noticed that Dylan was sitting on the round pen fence, watching her with the stallion. "When are you planning to saddle him?" she asked. "He doesn't mind the blanket. Maybe we should try just putting a saddle on him."

"If you think he's ready. He tolerates me okay now, but he loves you."

Sam rubbed Trouble's nose. "He's a great horse. I think it must have been a man who abused him. Otherwise, why is he so much calmer with me?"

"I think you're right and you being a woman is part of it. But there's more to it than that. He's been around other women and he still doesn't trust them like he does you."

Dylan got off the fence and came over to Sam and the

stallion. "I've been thinking about it. It's pretty simple, really. Trouble was abused. You've worked with abused women. You're a doctor, you're compassionate, plus you have a special affinity with and knowledge of abused women and how to help them. It's no wonder Trouble trusts you."

"It's an interesting theory."

"But you don't believe it."

She shrugged. "I don't believe it or disbelieve it. The answer isn't something you can prove."

Today Dylan looked like the quintessential cowboy. Since it was warm, he wore a flannel shirt with the sleeves rolled up and no coat. Add in the cowboy hat, jeans, boots and chaps and he looked like exactly what he was. A working cowboy.

"What? You're staring at me."

"You're wearing chaps. I don't remember seeing you wear chaps before."

"I was out in some rough country earlier. Not to mention the barbwire fence. I wear them when I think I'll need them. Why?"

She smiled and stepped closer, laying her hand on his chest. "I love a man in chaps. I think they're very—" she tugged his head down, kissed his cheek and whispered in his ear "—sexy."

He wrapped his arm around her waist. "Hell, if I'd known that I'd have worn them every time I saw you." He kissed her mouth, taking his time. "Aren't you about through working with Trouble for the day?"

"Yes." She turned around to look at the stallion and swallowed a cry. Very quietly, she said, "Dylan, Shadow's in here. I thought Trouble didn't like dogs."

Dylan looked at them. "I'll be damned. He hasn't shown any interest in any of the others. Obviously he likes Shadow. Swear to God they're talking to each other."

They'd had their noses together, sniffing and now Trouble was nickering and Shadow was making some kind of woofing sound and whining. Shadow rolled to his back in the classic belly-rub pose. Trouble looked at him for a minute, then lowered his nose and blew on the dog's belly. Shadow loved it.

Sam and Dylan exchanged *what the hell* glances. Finally, Dylan had enough and said, "Come on. They'll be here forever if we let them."

Sam led Trouble into the barn and back to his stall, with Shadow prancing happily beside him. Dylan kept him in with the other horses in the hopes of socializing him. Although he kept the two stallions at opposite ends of the barn. To Sam, the horse seemed happier and much calmer than when she'd first met him. While she and Dylan cooled him down and groomed him, Shadow curled up beside him and took a nap. When they finished they put him in his stall with fresh water, hay and a scoop of oats. With some difficulty, Sam managed to get Shadow to come with her back to the house.

Glory was just leaving as they came in. "Dinner's on the stove top. If you're not going to eat soon, you need to refrigerate it. I left heating instructions." To Sam she said, "Dylan is incapable of remembering how to reheat things. Last time I forgot to leave a note, he put the chicken spaghetti in the oven with the plastic wrap still on it."

"I was thinking about something else. Besides, the plastic scraped off."

Sam laughed. "He told me about the bread fiasco. I didn't realize there were more issues."

"The stories I could tell you. You two have fun," Glory said, slipping on her coat. "Good luck, cowboy," she added with a wink.

"Good luck with what?" Sam asked.

Dylan scowled. "Nothing. Glory is just being a pain in the ass."

"A pain in the ass who you'd find it hard to live without. For one thing, you'd starve if she didn't cook for you."

"Just because that's true doesn't mean she's not a pain. That's the problem with someone who's known you since you were born. They can harass you with impunity."

"Poor baby," she said, patting his cheek. "But you still haven't answered my question."

"I'll tell you later. Right now, I'm starving. What about you?"

She gave up, knowing Dylan well enough by now to realize he wouldn't talk until he felt like it. "I'm hungry too.

What did Glory make for tonight?"

"Chicken spaghetti. Which is why she told her little story about me and the plastic wrap." He washed his hands at the sink, then got out plates for both of them. "There's salad and French bread, too."

"Sounds wonderful." Sam fed Shadow, then washed up while Dylan got out the salad and popped the bread in the oven.

They ate by candlelight in the kitchen, drinking wine and with classical piano music playing in the background. "Is this music by anyone I know?" Sam asked him.

"Philip Wesley. He's an incredible pianist and composer. This is 'Moonlight and Jasmine'."

"It's gorgeous. So romantic."

He grinned. "That was the object. Are you finished?"

She nodded. "Except I'd like more wine."

"Are you staying the night or are you driving home?"

"Staying."

"Good. Then you can have all the wine you want."

"Pour me some and I'll take the dishes to the sink."

When she returned, Dylan grabbed her hand and tugged her down to sit in his lap. "I'm afraid I'll have to charge you a toll for that wine."

Her lips curved upward. She put her arms around his neck. "And what would that toll be?"

He pretended to think about it. "A kiss."

Sam kissed him, a brief, butterfly kiss to his mouth.

"What if I want more wine?"

"You'll have to kiss me again."

She kissed him, this time slipping her tongue inside his mouth and teasing him to return the kiss. He groaned and cupped her breast through her shirt. She squirmed on his lap and felt an immediate response. He pushed back his chair and she straddled him. Even through her jeans and his, she felt him, hard and ready.

It's always like this with him. He touches me and I melt. The thought worried her a little but then he was pushing her shirt up, slipping his hand beneath her bra and caressing her bare breast and she was wrestling to get his shirt off. All she could think about was having his hands on her, his fingers inside her, his mouth on hers.

Dylan stood and she wrapped her legs around him and locked her lips on his as he walked with her through the living room and on to his bedroom. Once there he tossed her on the bed and followed her down. They wrestled with clothes until they were both naked, or mostly so.

He reached for a condom and she took it from him, rolling it down over his cock, which was clearly ready for her. Instead of lying back, she pushed him onto his back, straddled him and guided him inside her, gasping as he filled her. She started the slow, sensuous ride, throwing her head back, gasping with pleasure as he filled his hands with her breasts. The sweet friction pushed her higher, tighter. He grasped her hips and brought her down as he thrust upward. She cried out as she hit the crescendo and shattered, collapsing on his chest. He said her name, pumping in and out until he spilled inside her in his own climax.

Chapter Seventeen

*S*HIT, DYLAN THOUGHT as he got out of bed to get rid of the condom. *Tell me it didn't—*

"The condom broke," Sam said.

"I'm sorry." What the hell else could he say?

"I won't get pregnant. I'm on the pill. Do I need to worry about anything else?"

"No. I've always used a condom. And believe it or not, I've never had one break before."

"Come here," she said.

He sat beside her on the bed. She sat up and kissed him. "I believe you. You don't need to worry about me, either."

He smiled. "I wasn't." If Sam had any concerns, she'd have told him before they ever had sex.

They took a shower together. After soaping each other, he kissed and licked his way down her beautiful body, laying his lips on every inch of her skin. When he was so hard he thought he'd die if he didn't get inside her soon, he picked her up and put her back against the wall, her legs spread wide around his hips. Her sex was completely open to him and so damn tempting. He didn't say anything. He looked at her, waiting for her decision.

"Yes," she said.

He thrust deep inside her, feeling her muscles contracting around him, her soft, silken heat caressing his bare cock. She made sounds of pleasure, which made him even hotter. He couldn't hold back for long, driving inside her again and again until he came with a roar.

They dried off and he gave her a shirt to wear. One of his T-shirts that did nothing to hide the gorgeous body beneath it. He pulled on his boxers. "Are you hungry? I'm sure there's dessert."

"Chocolate?"

Dylan laughed. "I don't know, but it's a possibility."

They found a chocolate cake Glory had made. He had to laugh at how much Sam was enjoying it. She closed her eyes after each bite and moaned with pleasure. Finally, he said, "I don't think I've ever seen anyone have an orgasm over food."

Sam opened her eyes and frowned at him. "Do not try to ruin this for me. I'm not having a food orgasm. I'm simply enjoying possibly the best chocolate cake I've ever eaten."

"Glory will be happy to know that."

Sam got up and took her empty plate to the sink. "Will you tell her for me? I have to leave early so I can drop off Shadow at my house and change my clothes."

"You could leave Shadow here. We'd take care of him."

She walked back to the table. "But then I'll have to come

get him after work. I'm not sure how late I'll be."

He reached for her hand and tugged her over to stand between his legs. "There's an easy way to solve this problem."

"What problem? You mean going back and forth?"

"You don't have to do that, you know. You could stay with me."

"Tomorrow night?"

"Every night."

"What?" She looked absolutely stunned.

"Move in with me."

She stared at him for a moment, then her expression changed from surprise to understanding. "This is about the knife and the note, isn't it? I told you I'm fine."

"That's not what this is about, although it's another good reason. Shadow likes it here too. I think he's going to be a big help with Trouble."

"I'm not moving in with you because my dog and your horse have decided they're BFFs."

"Then move in with me because you want to be with me."

"Oh, Dylan. You know I love being with you. But—"

He pulled her into his lap and kissed her thoroughly. "Damn it, Sam. I want you to live here because I'm in love with you. It has nothing to do with any of the shit that's been going on."

She raised an eyebrow. "Nothing?"

"Okay, maybe a little. But that isn't the main reason. I

love you," he repeated. "I want you to live with me."

He couldn't tell what she was thinking. She hadn't said she loved him. Maybe she didn't. Maybe what was for him slam, bam, crazy in love wasn't the same for her. Her expression softened. She took his face in her hands and kissed him. "We haven't been together very long."

"Long enough."

"I've never lived with anyone. Other than a roommate."

"Neither have I."

"I need to think about this. This isn't something I can decide on the spur of the moment."

While it wasn't the answer he'd wanted, it was a hell of a lot better than *no* or *absolutely not*. It wasn't unreasonable for her to want time to think about such a big change. Instead of answering, Dylan kissed her.

"What, no arguments?"

"Darlin', that is my argument." He stood with her in his arms and started toward the bedroom.

"Where are you taking me?"

He stopped walking and kissed her again. "Just making sure you know what you're missing."

She laughed. "And here I thought you'd argue."

"Making love is a lot more fun than arguing," he told her, tossed her on the bed and followed her down.

"You got that right," she murmured.

A COUPLE OF days after Dylan asked her to move in with him, Sam's cell phone rang as she was on her way out the door to go to work. Caller ID said it was the Marietta Police Department. "May?"

"Yes, it's me. Do you have a minute?"

"Just. Did you find out anything?"

"I did. I have possible good news and bad news. Which do you want first?"

"Possible good news? What does that mean?"

"We're ninety percent sure your stalker isn't Gary Baxter."

"Why ninety percent?"

"Not long after he was released he got into a feud with a drug dealer. He was tortured and killed. His body was dumped into Lake Grapevine, but it wasn't discovered for months. Because of the extent of the torture and the decomposition of the body, he couldn't be positively identified. But they believe it was Baxter."

"I don't know, May. It sounds like he could still be alive."

"They declined to do further testing. They're going with whatever evidence they had to prove his identity."

"Do you believe it's him?"

May hesitated. "I'm keeping an open mind. But I think it's worth looking into other possible suspects."

"What's the bad news?"

"The bad news is since he hasn't been positively identified, Baxter is still a suspect and we don't know who your stalker is."

"All in all, that sounds like shitty news to me."

"Not totally. I've been able to rule out a few of the men who are on that list you gave me. I have pictures of the others and I'm still working on the list, trying to rule out the remaining ones. They're digital so I can email them to you."

She should remember what they all looked like, but with the exception of two or three, their features kind of ran together. And even the ones she remembered she hadn't seen in quite a while. Honestly, she didn't believe she could have seen one of the men and not recognized him. But she admitted it was a possibility. "I was about to leave for work. Email me and I'll look at them when I have a chance." She gave May her email address.

"Got it. Do you have Dylan's email? He should look at these too, in case one of them is familiar to him. Or I can email him."

"Could you go ahead and email Dylan? I don't know when I'll manage to look at them, much less forward them." May agreed and Sam hung up, not holding out a lot of hope that the pictures would help her identify the man. At the very least he would have tried to hide his identity. It could be anyone in Marietta. *Anyone in Marietta who's watching you.* The man seemed to know a lot about her movements. Still, all he'd done was commit some vandalism and leave a threatening note. *Stuck in your door with a big-ass knife. Don't forget that.*

She called Dylan and told him what May had found out. "She'll be emailing the pictures to you as well. I'll be late again tonight, so I won't see you."

"Be careful," Dylan said. "I've got a bad feeling the next thing he does will be significantly worse."

"You worry too much." But all this waiting for the other shoe to drop gave her a bad feeling too. "I'll text you when I get home and if you're up you can call me."

"All right. I'll talk to you later. Be careful."

Sam made sure Shadow had food and water and let him out one last time. She was still too concerned about him to give him the freedom to go in and out while she was gone. For all she knew this pervert could try to poison her dog and she wasn't about to risk that.

"Be a good boy," she told him, with a last pat on the head.

She'd thought about having an alarm installed after Dylan suggested it. First of all, she thought that was overkill in a town like Marietta. Secondly, if she moved in with Dylan then she wouldn't need an alarm. She still hadn't made up her mind about that.

Dylan said he loved her. Was she being naive to believe him? Or was it more like wishful thinking? Sam had finally admitted, to herself, anyway, that she was in love with Dylan as much as he claimed to be with her. Something was keeping her from telling him. An overabundance of caution?

Or something else? Even if she did tell him her feelings, moving in together was a huge step that she wasn't quite ready for yet.

Chapter Eighteen

DYLAN WAS MUCKING out a stall when he heard his brother Wyatt's voice. "I thought you were the boss around here. Why is it every other time I see you, you're mucking out stalls?"

"Why don't you grab a shovel and help me instead of standing around being a smartass?"

"I'm not the one who wanted to be a rancher," Wyatt said mildly. But he picked up a shovel and started helping. "Seriously, where the hell are your ranch hands?"

"Connor, Al and Bret are bringing the horses in from the fields. I don't know where the hell Monroe is. He's supposed to be in here helping me."

"He not working out?"

Dylan leaned on the fork and grimaced. "Not so much. None of the other hands like him. Glory says his eyes are shifty. Half the time I can't find him. I'd fire him in a heartbeat if I knew Clay would be back soon. But he's still got treatments left, and he's going to be weak for a good while after that." He tried not to think about what would happen if the treatments didn't work.

"So fire him and hire someone else."

"I'm thinking about it." The guy had seemed awfully down and out when Dylan had hired him, but his work ethic left a lot to be desired.

"Rumor has it you and Sam are hot and heavy." Wyatt dumped manure into the wheelbarrow. "When's the wedding?"

Dylan knew Wyatt expected him to deny any thought of weddings. He obviously hadn't talked to Glory in the past week or so since Dylan had asked Sam to move in with him. He'd thought it best to warn Glory that Sam might move in rather than spring it on her out of the blue. After all, Sam would be another person for Glory to fret over and take care of. There's no way Glory could have kept that news a secret from Wyatt or any of his brothers. Dylan hadn't bothered to ask her not to tell them. He knew once he told one brother, all of them would know within an hour.

"There's no wedding."

"Surprise," Wyatt said dryly.

"I asked Sam to move in with me."

Wyatt stopped in mid-shovel. "You, the last Gallagher bachelor, asked a woman to move in with you? Are you kidding me?"

"I didn't ask just any woman. I asked Sam. She's thinking about it."

Wyatt stared at him. "You're serious. You asked Sam to

live with you?"

"I did."

"Is she going to?"

Dylan shrugged. "I think so. She says neither of us has ever lived with anyone, besides roommates or family, and we need to be sure."

Wyatt stopped shoveling, tilted his head and considered him. "Are you sure that's not just bullshit?"

"No. Goddamn it. How can I be? But Sam's as independent as they come, so I guess it shouldn't surprise me that it would take her a while to warm up to the idea. Hold on a minute." He propped his fork against the wall and left the stall to go out in the corridor.

He'd seen a flash of movement out of the corner of his eye. Sure enough, when he rounded the corner, there was Monroe, standing around like he had nothing to do.

"Having a nice break?"

"Oh, sorry, Boss. I've been raking the round pen. Is there something else you want me to do?"

Raking the round pen, his ass. He'd bet the man had done no more than push around a little horseshit. "You were supposed to be mucking out stalls while the horses were turned out."

Monroe looked at him blankly. Sometimes Dylan wondered if he had a brain or his head really was as empty as it seemed. Irritated as shit, he shook his head. "Never mind. Go finish up. My brother and I were working on Sunshine's stall."

"Gotcha, Boss." Dylan followed him to the stall, partly to make sure he did what he'd told him to do and partly to get Wyatt.

"Come on up to the house. We'll have a beer before you leave. There's something I need to talk to you about."

Once they were out of hearing distance, washing up at the sink, Wyatt said, "That's the new guy?"

"That's him."

"He sure gives off a weird vibe. He didn't say a word when he came into the stall. Just looked at me like I was a piece of horseshit that needed shoveling."

"Well…" He picked up a clean towel to dry his hands with.

Wyatt punched him in the arm.

Dylan laughed and tossed him the towel. As they walked to the house he said, "I'm worried about Sam."

"Worried she won't move in with you?"

"No, I think she will. Eventually." Dylan opened the kitchen door and walked in. Going to the refrigerator, he pulled out a couple of beers and handed one to Wyatt. "I just hope it's not too late."

"Too late? What does that mean?" Wyatt asked, following Dylan into the living room.

Dylan sat on the comfortable couch. Glory kept hinting they needed a new one, but that was low on Dylan's list of priorities. "Sam's got a stalker."

"The hell you say. When did that happen?"

"A few weeks ago. It started slow but it's been escalating." Dylan told Wyatt what had been going on, including why they thought the stalker was someone from Sam's past. "May Rogers is investigating. All we know so far is the most likely suspect is believed to be dead."

"Believed to be or is dead?"

"The Dallas cops think he's dead but there's been no positive ID. But he hasn't surfaced anywhere that they know of, so that's another reason to think he's dead.

"Damn. Are there other suspects?"

"Yes. Sam thinks there are several men she testified against who might have it in for her."

"Jesus. You can't even say for sure it's one of those people, can you?"

"No, but the note stuck to her door with a knife makes it a damn good possibility."

"That's true. What are you going to do?"

"Not much I can do. I suspect she'd be safer here, but hell, I can't guarantee it. Not to mention I can't force her to move in with me. And I can't go stay at her house for more than a night here and there, not with the ranch to take care of."

"Damn, Dylan. I hope they find out who it is before something worse happens."

"Amen to that."

SHIT. IT WOULD be easier to get at her at the ranch, although it was tough making sure she didn't see him. Still, he looked a lot different from the way she'd remember him. Especially with his colored contacts.

He'd been thinking hard about what to do next. Did he want to go ahead and take her out? Or scare the shit out of her some more?

He could set events in motion and see how it turned out. If she died, great. He could leave and go back to looking for his bitch of a wife. If not, he'd stick around until he thought of another way to make her pay.

Nobody fucks with me and mine and gets away with it. Nobody.

SAM GOT HOME late that night, barely having had a chance to sit down all day. She operated almost the entire time she was at the hospital. She was tired, hungry, and her feet hurt like hell from standing on the hard hospital floors all day. She let Shadow out, and went out back to watch him. It was late, so she texted Dylan rather than call him. If he wasn't asleep, she thought, he should be.

Her phone rang almost as soon as she sent the text. "Hi, Dylan. Why aren't you asleep?"

"Because I'm worried about you. I'm not trying to push you into something you aren't ready for, but I really wish you'd stay with me at the ranch."

She was wavering. Honestly, she wasn't sure what was

keeping her from saying yes. "Let's talk about it tomorrow. I'm going to bed as soon as I eat and feed Shadow. And yes, I've still got my gun in case someone tries to break in."

"I'll come to you."

"No, you won't. You're short-handed already. You can't afford to be over here babysitting me every night."

"Damn it."

"Admit it. You're needed at the ranch."

He didn't deny it. She knew he wasn't happy about not being with her, but he didn't argue any more. He probably knew it was pointless to argue about something she'd been so adamant about. She promised to talk to him in the morning and they hung up.

Shadow wanted to play, of course. Since he'd been cooped up all afternoon and part of the night, she didn't have the heart to disappoint him. He was doing great now. His leg had healed, he'd put on weight and he loved her madly. There was a lot to be said for the total adoration a dog could give his owner.

Most of the snow had melted in her backyard. She'd even seen a few flowers around town, pushing through the remnants of snow. Spring wasn't far off. She turned on the outside lights and threw the ball for half an hour, then took Shadow in and wiped him down, since he was pretty much a mud pie. She popped a frozen dinner in the microwave and while it heated, fed Shadow. Once she ate, she crawled into bed and fell asleep almost as soon as her head hit the pillow.

She awoke to Shadow barking loudly, then whimpering and nosing her. "What the hell—"

She heard a crash and the sound of glass breaking. Shadow growled and charged the window. Sam sat up and turned on the light, yelling at Shadow to come as she did. *Jesus. There's smoke everywhere. There's—oh, my God, what is that burning?* She jumped out of bed then stood there, coughing, trying to think as flames licked at the curtains and quickly ignited them. The smoke alarm started wailing. Returning to her, Shadow kept barking and nipping her pajama pants trying to herd her out. She grabbed a sweatshirt off the chair by the bedroom door. Peering out of the open bedroom door, she saw smoke but the flames were confined to her bedroom.

Yielding to Shadow's now frantic actions, she headed for the front door. As she passed it, she grabbed her purse, unlocked the front door and ran outside with Shadow glued to her side. As soon as they reached a safe distance, she stopped and turned around. Her stomach churned. To her it looked like the entire house was in flames.

She yanked her cell phone out of her purse and started to dial 9-1-1. Some of her neighbors had come outside and were watching and offering help. Kristin Northfield, who lived next door, said, "I called 9-1-1 when I heard your fire alarm go off. The fire department should be here any minute. Are you all right?"

"Yes." She pulled on her sweatshirt, then wrapped her

arms around herself, shivering. Whether from shock or the cold, she couldn't tell. "Shadow woke me up just before— just before—my God, Kristin, I didn't know what it was at first but someone threw a Molotov cocktail into my bedroom."

Kristin stared at her. "A Molotov cocktail? You mean a bomb? Someone threw a bomb in your window?"

"Yes."

"You'll have to tell the firefighters and the cops. In the meantime, you're bound to be freezing," Kristin said, practically. "Come to my house until the fire department gets here."

"No, I'm okay." She couldn't stop staring at her home. At the fire that was fast expanding. Her feet that were turning to icicles, no surprise considering she was barefoot. Shadow whimpered and she put her hand on his head. "Good boy. We're okay now." Thanks to Shadow.

"If you won't come inside I'm going to get you something warm," Kristin said. She returned a few minutes later with some thick socks, house shoes and a jacket.

"Thank you, Kristin."

"I still think you should come inside—"

The wail of sirens cut off her words. Moments later two police cars drove up, closely followed by a fire truck. Firefighters spilled out, readying their equipment, attaching a hose to the nearby fire hydrant. The fire captain searched her out, asking if there were any more people inside. "No, it was just me and my dog."

"That's good." He turned to leave.

"Captain, wait. It started in my bedroom, I think. Someone threw a bomb through the window. I know it sounds insane but—"

He cut her off. "We'll take care of it. One of the paramedics will be over to check you out shortly."

Sam didn't argue, knowing it was easier to let them check her than to fight about it. The scene was a madhouse, with onlookers, cops and firefighters everywhere, water streaming from the fire hose. The noise was deafening, from people shouting as well as the fire alarm and sirens still sounding.

She needed to call Dylan, if only to make sure he heard about the fire from her and knew she and Shadow were all right. More than that, though, she wanted to see him. Needed to see him. She went into Kristin's house to call, Shadow still sucked up against her like superglue.

"Dylan?"

"Sam?" He sounded groggy at first, then he snapped awake. "It's two a.m. What's wrong?"

"Someone threw a bomb through my bedroom window. My house is on fire."

Chapter Nineteen

HOLY SHIT! A BOMB? What the fuck? A bomb? Sam's house was on fire?

"Are you all right? Are you hurt?" His heart beat double time. *Calm down. If she was seriously hurt she wouldn't be calling. The hospital would.* He shook his head hard, trying to clear the image of Sam, injured—or worse.

"I'm okay and so is Shadow. Neither of us are hurt at all. The fire department is here and they're getting it under control."

"I'm coming over." He picked up his jeans and yanked them on. Grabbed a shirt and put it on.

He thought she might argue. Instead she said, "Thanks. I—oh, God, Dylan, it's horrible."

"I'll be there as soon as I can."

Dylan made it to Sam's house in record time. The street was blocked by police cars and the fire truck and firefighters were still there. He parked as close as he could and walked the rest of the way, finding Sam as soon as he drew near the house. Shadow was by her side and she wore a coat that was way too big for her, pajama pants and house shoes.

When she saw him she walked straight into his arms. He put his arms around her and hugged her, then kissed her. "Are you sure you aren't hurt?"

"Yes, I'm all right. Shadow woke me up right before anything happened. I guess he heard someone outside. They—he—he threw something through the window that exploded. Shadow got me out before the flames engulfed my bedroom."

Her bedroom. The son of a bitch had tossed a fucking bomb into her bedroom. He looked at the house. "Why are the firefighters on the roof? It looks like they're aiming their hoses—good God, did the hole in the roof come from the fire? Already?"

"No. They said they needed to cut a hole in the roof to be able to better get to my bedroom. The source of the fire."

She rested her hand on the dog's head. He was snugged up tight against her side and didn't look like he would leave her anytime soon.

Dylan patted Shadow's head. "Good boy."

"Thank God Shadow was with me. If he hadn't been— The bed was burning as I left the room. The fire chief says the fire is mostly confined to my bedroom, but the smoke damage is all over the house."

Dylan looked at the house again, his stomach turning at the thought of Sam being trapped inside with the fire raging. "You saw the bomb?"

"Yes. It looked homemade. Like a Molotov cocktail or something like that. I told the fire chief and May. She said she'd get more details later."

Shit! It really was a bomb. Which meant it was arson. And attempted murder. The bastard meant to kill her.

May caught up with them while the firefighters were finishing up. "Do you feel up to talking to me, Sam? We can wait until tomorrow if you'd rather."

"It's better if we talk while it's fresh in my mind, isn't it?" Sam asked.

"I don't think a few hours will make a difference."

"Let's do it now."

"Your neighbor offered her kitchen if you'd like to go there."

"That's sweet of her. Poor Kristin has been trying to get me to go inside for hours."

Before long Sam, Dylan, May and Shadow were all sitting around Kristin Northfield's kitchen table, drinking hot coffee. Kristin and her husband, Craig, were both there as well. Sam asked them to stay in case they could remember seeing anything suspicious and May had agreed, saying another policeman would canvass the other neighbors who were awake and the rest later in the day.

"It was a bomb, May," Sam said.

"Yes, it was. A homemade IED. The fire chief confirmed it. We'll have more details after they have a chance to thoroughly examine the scene. So let's start at the beginning.

You said you came home late tonight. Take me through that and what you did after you got home."

Sam had exchanged the jacket for a blanket her friend had given her. Her face was white and pinched, both from exhaustion and stress, Dylan figured. She took a sip of coffee and started.

"It was after eleven when I got home. I took Shadow out and we played ball for half an hour. With the lights on in the backyard. I didn't see anyone or anything unusual and I don't think Shadow did because I think—no, I know he would have alerted me to something like that.

"Then we came in, I microwaved a frozen dinner and went to bed. I guess it was around midnight or a little later."

"The 9-1-1 call came in at 1:42."

"That was me," Kristin volunteered. "I heard her smoke alarm go off and when I looked out the window to see what was going on I saw flames coming from Sam's house. So I called emergency."

"Shadow woke me up just before the bomb came through the window. He must have known he was outside."

"Did you know it was a bomb immediately?"

Her brows knit together. "I think so. Shadow had awakened me just a couple of minutes before I heard the window glass breaking. The window was screened, so he'd have had to get rid of that. Maybe that's what Shadow heard. Anyway, I saw a bottle with a burning rag stuffed into it. Isn't that a Molotov cocktail?"

"Sounds like it," May said.

"The curtains caught fire immediately and the bed was already going up by the time Shadow and I left the room." She reached for Shadow, who immediately put his head under her hand.

Dylan sat there trying to wrap his mind around the fact that the bastard who was after Sam had thrown a bomb into her bedroom. Talk about escalation. Draining the gas, slashing the tires, even the note stuck to the door with a knife, could all be counted as nuisances. But setting her home on fire—with a goddamn bomb—that was attempted murder.

"Is there anything else you can think of to tell me?" May asked.

Sam simply shook her head. May gave her a long look, then turned to Dylan with a questioning lift of her eyebrows. "She'll be staying with me," he told her, even though he and Sam hadn't discussed it yet. Sam didn't protest, which he took as either a good sign, or she hadn't been paying attention and was too upset to even think that far ahead.

"Good." May nodded decisively. "Mr. and Mrs. North-field, did you see or hear anything suspicious prior to hearing the alarm?"

Both of them said no and May continued, "Have you seen any unusual activity around Sam's house in the last few weeks?"

"I told them about the tires and the note," Sam said.

"Yes, we talked about it after she told us. Neither of us has seen anything out of the ordinary," Kristin said.

"I don't—" Sam's phone rang. She pulled it out of her purse and checked it. "It's Bianca. I need to take this." She got up and walked into the other room.

Dylan looked at May. "Can I talk to you?"

Craig said, "If you need us we'll be in the living room. Come on, Kristin."

As soon as they walked out, Dylan said, "It's him. Her stalker."

"We can't say that for certain, Dylan. That's quite an escalation."

"Exactly. Discounting the first two things, the note was threatening and now her home was set on fire. Attempted murder. If it's not her stalker then who the hell is it?"

"We're investigating, Dylan."

"That's all you're going to say?"

May pressed her lips together. "Yes, it's likely to be the same person who's been harassing her. But we have no physical evidence yet to back that up. The suspect has to arise out of the evidence if we want an arrest. Not the other way around. You don't pick the suspect and then try to make the evidence fit." May leaned forward and pinned him with what he thought of as her 'cop stare'. "Don't go around saying the cops think he did it, either. That could prejudice the case when we do catch him."

"You don't have to worry, May. I get it." He didn't like

it, but he understood it. Still, he needed to tell his brothers what had happened and he saw no reason not to tell them who he suspected. They'd keep it to themselves if he asked them to.

After May left, he called the hospital to see if any of his brothers were on call and in the hospital. Sean came on the line shortly.

"What's going on, Dylan? There's a rumor that Sam's house is on fire."

"It's no rumor, it's true."

"The hell you say! Was Sam there?"

"Yes, but she's all right." He told him what had happened and what they knew or believed.

"Thank God the dog got her up in time for her to get out. Is there anything Honey or I can do?"

"Yeah, you can tell Jack, Wyatt and the wives later this morning. No sense waking them up. Oh, and tell Glory too."

"I'll do that. Tell Sam I'm glad she's okay. I can talk to the other trauma surgeons about covering for her if she needs me to."

"Thanks. I'll let her know."

OBVIOUSLY, BIANCA HAD heard about the fire or she wouldn't have called Sam in the middle of the night when she knew Sam wasn't working.

"Oh, my God, Sam. I just heard there's a fire at your house. Are you all right?"

"I'm okay, Bianca."

"You're sure? Was anyone hurt?"

"No, I'm all right and no one was hurt. But the fire—my bedroom is on fire." Sam closed her eyes, seeing her bedroom, burning as she left it. "I'm next door at Kristin's. The fire department is here. I don't know how long they'll be here putting it out."

"Do you want me to come over? Oh, forget that. I'm coming over."

Before she could protest, Bianca hung up.

Ten minutes later her friend rushed into Kristin's house and immediately grabbed Sam in a tight hug. "I'm so thankful you're all right."

Sam blinked back tears. Bianca, who knew her well, held her away and snapped, "Don't you dare cry or I'll cry too. You know I hate to cry."

What she really meant was that Bianca knew Sam hated to cry. "I wouldn't dream of it," she told her friend.

It was near dawn by the time the fire department pronounced the fire extinguished and allowed them to go in. Sam had forced Bianca to leave since she had work that day. Dylan tried to get Sam to leave before the fire was out, but she meant to stay until the bitter end.

"Damn, you're stubborn," he said.

"Like you're not?"

He shrugged and followed her into the house.

Stomach churning, Sam stared at the wreckage of her bedroom. The thought that she might have been trapped inside scared the shit out of her. Shadow, still true to his name, had only left her side twice since he'd awakened her. He hadn't gone far and he'd kept her in sight even then. The firemen told her they believed that in addition to the home-made bomb thrown inside, another had been thrown at the bedroom's outside wall. The wall was partially destroyed and the rest of the room was a near total disaster.

She couldn't look at her bed without wanting to throw up. Somehow, her closet had been spared, but all of the furniture had burned to some degree. There would be water damage throughout the house, particularly the bedroom. She knew everything in the house would reek of smoke. Opening up one of the plastic bags Kristin had given her, she didn't even attempt to get anything from the charred dresser. Instead she started in her closet.

"What can I do to help?" Dylan asked.

"Help me put some of the stuff from my closet in a bag." She handed him another plastic trash bag. "Jeans, shirts, boots, tennis shoes, scrubs. Basically whatever will fit in the bags. I'll need to pick up some baking soda and some other supplies to get the smell out of my clothes." She knew about baking soda, but she'd have to read up on what else to do to get rid of the smoke smell.

"Were you supposed to work today?" he asked, beginning to sort through the closet.

"Yes, but I called the hospital and told them what happened. The schedulers said they'd take care of finding someone to work for me."

"For how long? I suspect you'll need a few days, at least."

"They'll do their best but I'd be surprised if I can get off for more than a couple of days."

"Sean said he'd talk to some people about pitching in for you."

"That's sweet of him. Thank him for me."

"Are you supposed to talk to the fire inspector later?"

"Yes. He's supposed to call me."

"Maybe he'll be able to identify who did it."

"We know who did it. The same man who left that note."

"May said they need proof. Physical evidence that points to a suspect. And not to talk about it, either."

"I know. She told me the same thing." *A bomb. Attempted murder. God, what next?* "May said the police will have someone watch the house until after the fire inspector does his thing. I don't know what I'm supposed to do when the cops finish with it. The damage to the outside wall leaves my bedroom wide open for any vandal or looter who wants in."

"Luckily, there aren't a lot of those in Marietta." Dylan walked over to her. "Maybe you can hire a night watchman until it can be repaired. We'll figure it out."

"I know." Fighting tears, she swallowed hard. She

couldn't remember the last time she really cried. It wasn't that she didn't feel things. She did, sometimes too much. But her job was such that she couldn't afford to cry whenever something went wrong, or someone died, or anything bad happened. Those situations came up too often. No one wanted a trauma surgeon who couldn't hold her shit together.

That frame of mind spilled over into her personal life.

Dylan pulled her into his arms and hugged her. "Sam, it's okay to be upset. You don't have to be so stoic."

She put her arms around his waist and rested her head against his chest. God, she wished she could let go. But she couldn't. She didn't dare. "Yes, I do."

He rubbed her back comfortingly. "Why? There's no one else here but me. And I sure as hell won't hold it against you."

"Because…it's the only way I can function. I need to be in control of my emotions. I'm a surgeon, Dylan. I can't afford to—to fall apart."

He didn't say anything at first, just looked down at her, frowning. Then he said, "You're not at the hospital. You're not performing surgery. You're a woman whose home was set on fire by a fucking maniac with a bomb. You're entitled to feel whatever you feel."

"Of course I feel it! Just because I'm not breaking down in tears doesn't mean I'm not sickened and scared about what the son of a bitch is planning next." She pushed herself away from him and went back to tossing things into the bag. "Who the hell could it be?"

"Didn't you say May emailed you some pictures of suspects?"

She nodded. "I haven't had a chance to look at them."

"We can do that after you get some sleep. Where's your computer?"

"In the den, I think. I've got my tablet in my purse."

"Why don't you go get your computer and whatever else you need from the rest of the house and put it in a pile? I can finish gathering your clothes while you do that."

"All right. Dylan?" He looked at her. "Thank you for being here."

"You don't need to thank me. I love you. Where else would I be?"

"I'm a very lucky woman."

He gave a wry laugh. "First time I've heard having a stalker described as being lucky."

"Not that. But I'm lucky to have you." She kissed him and left to gather her things. The knot in her stomach wouldn't disappear until they caught the man who'd done this. But until then, what new hell would he come up with since his plan to burn her alive hadn't worked?

Chapter Twenty

LATER THAT EVENING Dylan and Sam were finally able to sit down and look at the pictures of the suspects that May had emailed to Sam. He'd been busy with the ranch chores and as far as he could tell, Sam hadn't sat down all day. She'd spent the day going back and forth between the ranch and her house. And she'd been on the phone nonstop too. Neither of them had gotten any sleep, and though Sam maintained she was accustomed to sleepless nights occasionally, Dylan thought she looked fragile enough to break.

He didn't like it. He hated seeing her so upset, and knowing there was nothing he could do to help her. Sam was one of the strongest women he'd ever known, but the fact that some crazy had set a fire in order to kill or maim her had done a number on her. Not that she'd admit it.

They ate a late dinner that Glory had left for them.

"Poor Shadow," Sam said, glancing at him curled up on the floor beside her. "If I'm anywhere near him he won't leave my side. And Glory said he frets whenever I leave him."

"He's protecting you."

She reached down to stroke his head. "He sure did. You told me he'd protect me before I ever took him home. I couldn't imagine why I'd need protection."

"I didn't think you'd need it either. But Shadow seemed like a loyal dog, and he is." Thank God. Changing the subject, he asked, "Do you want a glass of wine with dinner?"

"I'd better not. I'd probably fall asleep in my plate."

"You can have one before bed, then."

"Okay." They ate in silence for a bit then Sam said, "I talked to the arson investigator earlier. He questioned me, not that I think anything I told him helped. The bomb makes it clear the cause was arson, not accidental. He should receive word on the samples he sent off of the bomb and the accelerants used."

"That's something, I guess. Have you talked to May again?"

"Yes. She didn't say anything new. Just that they're investigating and not to talk to anyone but the police and my insurance company about the fire. I'm to send the insurance company a police report of the fire."

Noticing Sam was looking more drawn and tired by the minute, Dylan said, "We don't have to look at those pictures tonight. You need sleep."

"No, I want to get it over with. I don't expect we've seen any of these suspects around Marietta. But we have to look."

He didn't argue. Partly because there was no point to it

and partly because he thought it might make her sleep easier anyway.

May had sent seven pictures of possible suspects along with a picture of Gary Baxter, the murderer who was presumed dead. They looked through the digital pictures together. None of them sparked any instant recognition. Disappointing, even though neither had expected that to happen.

Dylan picked out one of the seven pictures and said, "Something about this one is familiar, but I can't put my finger on it."

"Let me mag it up." She did so and they both stared at the picture.

He looked like a mountain man. One who hadn't seen a razor or a bath in months. Long, brown, bushy hair, a mustache and full beard was an effective screen for what he really looked like. His eyes, a strange silver color, held an insolent gleam, and his posture, even in a mug shot, was arrogant. Dylan could easily see the man beating up a woman or a child and enjoying it.

Sam peered at the picture and frowned. "That's Bill Wade. He went to prison for domestic violence and assault. Not too long before the Baxter case. He didn't quite manage to kill his wife, but it sure as hell wasn't for lack of trying," she added. "From what I understand, his wife, ex-wife, rather, managed to disappear during the time he was in prison. I testified against him, so he could easily have it in for me."

"Have you seen him anywhere in Marietta?"

She shook her head regretfully. "No. He'd be hard to miss if he still looks like that. Not to mention his eyes are distinctive." She shivered, which she tried to cover up.

"Maybe he doesn't. He could have changed his appearance."

Sam shut down the computer. "He could have, I guess. Hopefully it will come to you why he looks familiar. In the meantime, I've got to get some sleep."

"I'm with you there."

As TIRED AS she was, Sam had thought she'd go right to sleep. No such luck. Dylan held her in his arms spooned together, back to front. Every now and then she thought he kissed the top of her head, though it was so gentle a touch she could be imagining it. Closing her eyes, she sought sleep again. Instead scene after scene of fire, smoke, sirens and the charred remains of most of her bedroom flashed through her mind.

"Dylan? Are you asleep?"

"No. But I thought you were. You're bound to be exhausted."

"I am." Beyond exhausted. "Every time I close my eyes I relive those first moments after Shadow woke me. The sound of the breaking glass, the fire from the bomb, and then when

I turned on the light, smoke, fire and pure paralyzing fear. If it hadn't been for Shadow I'm not sure I'd have gotten out of the bedroom in time."

"Yes, you would have. But thank God for Shadow all the same." His arms tightened around her. He kissed the top of her head. "I can't sleep either. Seeing your house, especially your bedroom, brought it home to me how close I came to losing you."

She turned in his arms and kissed him. "Make love to me, Dylan," she whispered, and kissed him again.

He pushed up the T-shirt she'd worn to bed and slipped it off over her head. He kissed her lips, the slow, deliberate thrusts of his tongue into her mouth mimicking the final act. Licking, kissing, he worked his way down her neck to her breasts, teasing and caressing each one until her nipples were hard, begging for more. Sam tugged on his hair, saying, "Kiss me."

He kissed her mouth, long and slow, arousing in itself.

"Now just lie back and let me love you," he said. She tangled her fingers in his hair and let him work his magic.

He moved down her body, licking, sucking, kissing. Her back arched, her hips bucked as his fingers toyed with her, dipped inside her, played with her. She did what he'd asked, letting him arouse her, take her on a sensuous journey into oblivion. His mouth took the place of his fingers, teased her until she came, screaming.

He thrust into her swollen flesh with long, driving

strokes, faster and faster, her hands clutching his butt, pulling him ever closer until he drove into her a final time and came deep inside her.

After a while, he rolled to his side, taking her with him. They slept in each other's arms, tangled up in each other for the remainder of the night. In the morning she woke to Dylan's kisses, his hands caressing her. Before long he was above her, sliding inside her, riding her gently until she climaxed as if in a dream.

"Am I awake?" she wondered aloud.

"I'm pretty sure you are," he said, chuckling.

"Dylan?" She wrapped her arms around his neck and kissed him. Then pulled back to look into his eyes, mossy green and full of tenderness. "I love you."

DYLAN STARED AT Sam. Did she mean it? Did she really love him or did she just *think* she did because she was glad to be alive?

"Yes, I mean it. I wouldn't have said it otherwise."

"I didn't realize I was so easy to read."

"To me you are." She kissed him again. "And I really do love you. I have for a while now."

He took her face in his hands and kissed her. "I love you too."

"Much as I'd love to stay here, I have a wad of people to meet at my house." Sam got out of bed and disappeared into the bathroom. A few minutes later he heard the shower come on.

He got up and pulled on his jeans to take Shadow out. He'd been whining for a while now. Dylan was fairly certain that any attempt to separate Shadow from Sam for bedtime would be a complete waste of time. A good thing, really, since the dog had already proved himself by getting her out of that fire.

Who the hell was out to get her? Damn it, he should be able to protect her, but he couldn't. He smiled a little. She'd be the first to say she could take care of herself and wouldn't especially welcome him hovering over her.

But now she was living with him. He wished it had been voluntary rather than necessary, but he'd take it whichever way it happened.

Dylan took Shadow out then left him in the kitchen with Glory while he went back upstairs to get dressed.

Sam was just finishing getting dressed. "I heard some good news yesterday, but I never had time to tell you. And then the fire put everything else out of my head."

"No surprise there. What's the news about?"

"Gretchen Hoffman. The people at the women's shelter where she went after she left the hospital were able to help her find a job in another city."

"That's great. So she hasn't gone back to the son of a bitch."

"Far from it. I think she's left the state, although they

wouldn't tell me where she went. And she filed for divorce."

"Are you surprised?" Dylan asked her.

"A little bit. She seemed unsure what she wanted to do, even after what she'd been through. What about you?"

"Definitely. After you told me the statistics of how many women go back to their abusers, I've been worried as hell that Gretchen would become one of those statistics."

"Fortunately, she didn't. Because of you."

"Me? You're the one who got her to the hospital and convinced her to give the women's shelter a try."

"But you're the one she called. You're the person she turned to. And you didn't let her down."

"You're giving me too much credit. We both helped her."

"I don't have time to argue about who helped her more. We'll call it a draw." She sucked in a breath and squared her shoulders. "I'm going to the house. Is it all right if I leave Shadow here?"

"Of course." He walked to her and tipped up her chin, looking into her eyes. "Will you be okay? I can come with you if you want."

She reached up to touch his cheek. "I really appreciate the offer but I know you have a lot to do here. I'll be fine."

He pulled her close and kissed her. "Call me if you need me. I have people who can handle things here if I need them to."

Chapter Twenty-One

I N THE TWO weeks since the fire and Sam moving in, Shadow and Trouble had grown even closer. The dog and the stallion clearly had a special bond. When she wasn't working at the hospital, Sam usually took Shadow with her. But since she worked a lot that left Shadow with Dylan a good bit of the time. He liked Dylan fine, got along well with the rest of the dogs, horses, barn cats and other assorted animals and people.

But he flat-out adored Sam and Trouble. Dylan had worried a little at first that without Sam around Shadow might run off, but he needn't have worried. The dog apparently knew a good thing when he had it.

Sam hadn't had much free time to spend with Trouble, but something had mellowed the stallion. Dylan suspected it was his bond with the dog that had done it, or certainly contributed. At any rate, Trouble allowed Dylan to start training him. When Shadow was around the horse was as gentle as a lamb. One afternoon Dylan left Trouble in the round pen with Connor and Shadow in his usual spot nearby while he went to the tack room to get a lightweight saddle to try on the horse. He'd just gone inside when he heard the door open.

"Hey, I wondered where you were. Connor said he thought you'd come in here."

Sam came in, shutting the door behind her.

"Hi. I didn't expect to see you back this early. Not that I mind," he added, pulling her into his arms and kissing her. It didn't take long until he thought about doing a lot more than just kissing. Sam put her arms around his neck and leaned in to him. She must have come straight from the hospital because she still wore her scrubs. He slid one hand over her butt and pulled her closer. "I missed you."

Sam laughed but didn't move away. "We saw each other this morning."

"So? Morning was a long time ago." He reached behind her and locked the door.

"Don't you have work to do?"

"Nothing that can't wait." He slipped a hand beneath her scrub top and rubbed her breast through her bra. They kissed, tongues tangling, straining against each other. "I want you," he told her, pushing her top up and pulling it off over her head before tossing it aside.

Her hand was rubbing his cock through his jeans. "I could kind of tell." Since she'd started unbuckling and unzipping him, he took that as assent. He boosted her up and she wrapped her legs around him, while she still tried to work her hand down inside his boxers. He sucked in a breath when she found bare skin.

Looking around for a place to sit, he spied a wooden chair. He carried her over to it, let her slide down his body, wringing a groan from both of them.

"Take these off," she said, trying to push his jeans down his legs.

"You first."

She stood back, untied her scrubs, let them drop and stepped out of them. Dylan managed to yank off his boots and push his jeans and boxers down and off. Sam pushed him back to sit on the chair and he helped her climb on top of him. "You still have on your panties."

Sam kissed him, rubbed her delectable body against him. He was hard and hot and wanted her right now. Wanted to drive inside her again and again, deep inside with her heat and her sheath gripping him tight, milking him until he came.

Instead of taking off her panties, she pushed them aside and sank down on him, drawing him in, riding him to a crescendo. He came like a geyser and she followed moments after, with a soft cry against his neck.

"Good God," was all he could manage.

"My thoughts, exactly." She climbed off of him and looked around for her clothes.

He began to get dressed. "I need to get back to Trouble. I'm supposed to be picking up a saddle." Although he figured Connor had a pretty good idea what could be taking him so long.

"They were fine right before I came in. He and Connor look like they're getting along pretty well." She gathered up her scrubs and put them on. "I don't think it's been very long."

Buckling his belt, he grinned and started to agree when he heard a commotion from outside. Yanking open the door, he went out to the round pen where all the noise was coming from.

Complete chaos met his eyes. The noise was deafening—shouting, neighing, barking all contributed. Connor and Al were both in the round pen. Obviously spooked, Trouble was rearing and Connor was hanging on to the lead rope, doing his best to calm down the horse without getting killed. In front of Trouble, in a protective stance from something unseen, was Shadow, snarling, barking and growling. Al held on to his collar with difficulty, restraining him from going after God knew what.

"What the hell is going on?"

SAM BARELY HAD time to take in the scene before Shadow broke free from the ranch hand who was attempting to hold him. The dog scrambled under the fence and took off down the barn's stone walkway.

"Shadow, come!"

He didn't even pause. She yelled the command again. Already three-fourths of the way down the aisle, Shadow slowed, stopped and turned to look at her. Obviously reluctant to let his prey go free, he looked behind him several times. Of course, she had no idea what he was going after. He whined as if asking if he could go.

"Come, Shadow."

Very slowly, he walked back to her, whimpering and growling as he continued to look back over his shoulder. When he reached her, he sat and looked pitiful.

Sam knelt beside him, patted his head and talked softly and calmly to him. "Good boy, Shadow. What's got you so upset?"

He whimpered and looked at the walkway. Sam saw a flash of movement and barely had time to grab him before Shadow took off again.

While she was taking care of Shadow, Dylan had gone to Trouble. Connor had left the horse to Dylan and stood nearby, shaking his head. The stallion was quivering and sweating, but he'd stopped rearing up and seemed to be listening to Dylan, who was talking to him softly.

The other ranch hand had come out of the pen to talk to her. "I'm sorry, ma'am. I couldn't hold him. That dog is stronger than he looks."

"Yes, he is. It's not your fault. Al, isn't it?"

"Yes, ma'am."

"What the hell happened here?" Dylan asked, but he said

it quietly so as not to upset the horse further.

Connor and Al both started talking at once.

"One at a time," Dylan interrupted. "Connor?"

"It was the damnedest thing, Boss. I was out here with Trouble and Al was cleaning the stalls. I saw Jim and told him to bring me a rake. Well, the minute Jim came near us, Shadow started barking and going batshit crazy. He got in front of Trouble like he was gonna protect him, or maybe both of us. Anyway, Trouble started freaking out too."

Al took over. "By the time I got out here Shadow was freaking out and looked ready to go after Jim. Like he couldn't decide between protecting the horse and taking a bite out of Jim. Damned if Jim didn't just stand there smiling. Swear to God, Boss, he was egging the dog on."

Connor interjected, "I yelled at him, asked him what the hell he thought he was doing, upsetting the animals like that. I had my hands full, trying to calm down Trouble, so I didn't hear what he said."

"But I did," Al said. "He was cussing the dog. Told him to come and get him, but the way he was holding that rake, I was afraid he'd skewer Shadow with it. So I grabbed a hold of the dog before he got hurt." He cast an apologetic glance at Sam. "Jim coulda just been talking, probably was, but I know how much you love that dog, ma'am."

"You did exactly right, Al. Thank you for protecting him."

Connor continued, "Al grabbed Shadow and I was still

hanging on to Trouble and while we were trying to calm them down, damned if the son of a bitch didn't take off."

"Took off where?"

"That way," Al said, pointing toward the barn.

"What the hell did he do to Shadow? I knew Burt didn't like him but I've never seen him around Shadow."

"That's because he usually stays out of Shadow's way," Connor said. "Him and Shadow were having it out one day not too long ago. Jim had a shovel and I swear to God, if I hadn't been there I think he'd have hit him with it."

"Sam, can you come hold Trouble while I look him over?"

She opened the gate to the round pen and Shadow followed her inside. Taking hold of Trouble's halter, she talked soothingly to him while Dylan checked him over.

"He's okay. Physically, anyway."

"What are you going to do, Boss?" Connor asked.

Dylan looked angrier than she'd ever seen him. "Do? I'm going to fire his ass. I can't keep a ranch hand that my animals hate. How do I know he hasn't been abusing them?"

"It does seem odd that Shadow's taken such a dislike to him," Sam said. "Unless he's given him reason." She hadn't noticed Shadow acting like he was hurt. But she'd been awfully busy, especially since the fire. And Shadow had spent a good portion of time with Dylan instead of her. Could she simply have missed it?

DAMNED DOG. HE should've taken care of it long ago. But Jesus, who knew the son of a bitch would freak out just seeing him? He hadn't touched the damn thing. Of course, if that dipshit Connor hadn't showed up he'd have taught the animal a lesson. Still, why did it flip out? The dog couldn't know that he'd been the one to set the fire. Not unless it had ESP.

Shit. Maybe it had smelled him. Whatever. Just to be safe, he'd keep out of the bitch's sight. He was fairly sure she wouldn't recognize him, but why take the chance?

Now, how was he going to take care of the bitch? The fire hadn't worked, more's the pity. He could try to cut her brake line, but that wouldn't necessarily kill her, or even hurt her. Same for trying to make the horse she rode have an accident. Not a sure thing. And he wanted a surefire way to get rid of her.

She had to die.

Chapter Twenty-Two

IT DIDN'T TAKE Dylan long to track down Jim Monroe. He was getting in his truck. "Going somewhere, Monroe?"

"I was looking for you. Thought I'd go up to the house."

"No, I was in the round pen trying to calm down my animals. What the fuck is the matter with you?"

"Me? That goddamn dog would've killed me if he got to me. And if he didn't, the horse would've. I didn't do anything wrong."

"That's debatable. According to Connor, you and Shadow have tangled before. Makes me wonder what you did for him to respond that way."

"Not a fucking thing. You're going to believe that dipshit Connor? He's had it in for me since I got here."

"Apparently he had reason. I'm thinking Shadow does too."

"He's got a reason all right. That animal's crazy. You need to get rid of it."

Dylan stared at him, wondering if he was serious. "Are

you shitting me? How about I get rid of you instead?"

"What do you mean, get rid of me?"

"You're fired, Monroe. I'll pay you for the rest of the week but you're done here."

Monroe stared at him with his mouth hanging open. Then his expression changed to anger. "You're firing me because of a goddamn dog? You can't do that."

"Watch me. Besides, Shadow isn't the only reason, he's just the catalyst." Being short a man was bound to be better than paying this asshole to do nothing. "You don't do shit. You're gone half the time and when you are here you're either half-assing whatever job I asked you to do or you're standing around with your thumb up your butt."

"That's a damn lie. I've worked hard here."

"We must have completely different definitions of hard work."

"You'll be sorry for this."

"No, I won't be. Come by the office and I'll cut you a check before you leave." He started to walk off, then turned around and added, "By the way, Burt doesn't like you either."

"Who the hell is Burt?"

"The big mixed breed we call the barn dog. The one who's always with the horses." He turned his back, grinning when he heard the man cursing. He should have fired him a while ago. To be honest, he'd been worried almost from the beginning, since Connor had taken such a dislike to him.

Connor had pretty good instincts about people.

He went to the office and wrote out the check immediately. The sooner Jim Monroe left, the better. A few minutes later, his soon to be ex-employee, came in.

"I ought to sue you," he said belligerently.

"For what? You haven't been here long enough to collect unemployment." He handed him the check.

"Because of that goddamn dog."

"Did he bite you?"

Monroe hesitated. "Not exactly."

"Let me know when you find a lawyer to take that case. Suing someone over a dog who barked at you isn't going to have lawyers falling all over themselves to help you."

Monroe snarled something under his breath. Probably "fuck you" if he had to take a guess. He jerked open the door and Sam stumbled into him.

"Oh, I'm—" Sam started to say but halted mid-sentence. They stared at each other for a long moment, then Monroe shoved her aside and went out the door.

Dylan was beside her in an instant. "Goddamn it, what's the matter with him? Are you okay, Sam?"

She rubbed her arm, where she had hit the door when he shoved her. "I'm fine. I take it that was Jim."

"How'd you guess? Yeah, that's him."

"When I ran into him I had the strangest feeling. He—It sounds melodramatic but I swear he radiated hate."

"I believe it. He's pissed as hell. I just fired him."

"I thought you were just talking when you said that. Don't you need him since Clay is still in treatment for his cancer?"

"I need someone. Monroe has been pretty damn useless. None of the hands like him and obviously Shadow hates him."

"Do you think we overreacted? I mean, Shadow's a dog. Maybe Monroe reminds him of someone who scared him."

"You heard what Connor said about the two of them getting into it before. I'm not taking a chance that the son of a bitch will hurt one of my dogs. Or my horses. Burt doesn't like him either. I don't know why he wanted to work on a ranch when it's obvious he doesn't even like animals."

"Dylan, is that why you told him you fired him? Because the dogs don't like him?"

Dylan shrugged. "Yeah, so?" Sam simply stared at him and he laughed. "Don't worry. I gave him other reasons too."

"No wonder he's so pissed."

Dylan drew her close and kissed her. "We've wasted enough time on Jim Monroe. Let's go tend to our animals."

THE NEXT DAY Sam got a call from May when she was in surgery. She called her back as soon as she could. After exchanging greetings she asked, "Have you found something new?"

"Not exactly knew, but we can rule out one of the suspects. Gary Baxter's body was positively identified. They ran a DNA test. Don't ask me why they didn't do that in the first place, but they didn't."

Sam pulled off her scrub cap and tossed it on the table in the doctors' lounge. "So it isn't Baxter."

"No. We're back to the other suspect list. Unless you've thought of anyone to add."

"No one."

"All right. Of the seven other suspects, the ones I sent you pictures of, four of them have alibied out. We can't find the remaining three. Rand Lewis, Bill Wade, and Arthur Fitz."

"I'll look at those three again, but I'm not holding out a lot of hope."

"I know it may not seem like it, but we're doing everything we can to find out who the arsonist is and arrest him."

"I'm sure you are, but you can't guarantee you'll find him, much less when you'll find him."

"The department is on it, Sam. I'm on it."

"And I appreciate that. I really do. But May—" Sam asked her the question that had worried her for some time, but especially since the fire. "He's not finished, is he? He won't stop until he's killed me."

"We can't be certain that's his goal. He might be trying to scare you and didn't necessarily mean to harm you."

"You don't believe that." In Sam's mind, anyone who would set fire to someone's house was intent on harming that person.

May sighed. "No. Unfortunately, the escalation from acts that could be classified as pranks to arson is especially concerning."

"He won't stop unless we can stop him first. Do you think Dylan's in danger?"

May hesitated. "It's possible."

"More than possible, isn't it?"

"Sam—"

"Never mind, I know I'm right. I'm moving out. I'm not going to put Dylan and everyone at the ranch in danger more than I already have."

"Sam, you can't live in your house. Where are you going to go?"

"I'll figure something out."

"Dylan's going to have something to say about that."

That was undoubtedly true. "It's not Dylan's decision. It's mine and I'm not willing to risk his safety. Or worse, his life."

"You let me know how that works out," May said wryly. "I've known Dylan since we were six years old. Something tells me he's not going to be down with you leaving, especially while you're in danger."

We'll see about that. Sam hung up, resolving to talk to Dylan the moment she got back to the ranch.

On her way out she ran into Bianca. "I'm glad we ran into each other. Want to have a drink? I feel like we haven't talked in forever."

Sam started to say no, but Bianca was right and they hadn't talked for more than a few minutes since the fire. Besides, she definitely needed a friend to talk to. Bianca not only knew what had been happening in Marietta, she knew all about what had occurred in Dallas. "Okay, but I can't stay long. I need to get back to the ranch."

They went to Grey's and got a table in the corner, out of the way. Once they ordered and had their drinks Bianca said, "What's wrong? Besides the fact that a crazy person is after you and burned down half your house."

"Isn't that enough?"

"For most people. But I sense something else is going on."

Sam fiddled with her drink before taking a sip. "Dylan could be in danger. Living with him—I shouldn't have done it. Hell, you could be in danger just from talking to me."

"That seems a tad melodramatic."

"So's a fire."

"Good point. But what can you do about it?"

"Move out. Break up."

Bianca stared at her. "Dylan's not going to go for that."

Irritated, Sam snapped, "I'm aware. May said the same thing. But it isn't up to Dylan, it's up to me."

"Is this an excuse because you feel like you're getting too close to him? You've started to care too much so you're pulling back?"

"No, it's because I don't want Dylan to be hurt."

Bianca looked at her skeptically, then took a drink and said, "Let's leave that aside for a moment."

"Gladly."

"How many suspects do the police have?"

"Two of my patients' husbands and one patient's significant other. But there's no physical evidence on any of them. Other than the note, and forensics didn't get anything from it. It does indicate it's someone from my past, but that's all it does."

"Let me look at their pictures. Maybe I've seen one of them."

Sam doubted it but got out her tablet, pulled up the pictures and handed it to her friend.

Bianca stared at them, then shook her head regretfully and gave the tablet back. "I've never seen any of them."

"I'd have been surprised if you had." She tucked the tablet away. "I know what I should do, but it won't be easy."

"Hmm. Let the police handle it. If I were you I'd go home and jump Dylan's bones, and try to forget about all this."

Sam had to laugh. "You would not. You worry more than I do when things go wrong." Bianca merely shrugged. "Speaking of love lives, what's going on with yours?"

Her friend's face clouded. "Nothing. Zero. Zip. Nada."

"Weren't you dating the guy who was with you at your birthday party? What's his name?"

"His name is 'piece of shit'. He is off my list forever."

"What did he do?"

"Nothing much. Just pretended he wasn't married. When I figured it out and called him on it, he tried to convince me that we had the real thing and besides, he was divorcing her as soon as he could. Yada, yada. The slug."

"I'm sorry, Bianca."

"I did get a little satisfaction. I was having a glass of red wine at the time. I tossed it in his face. I laugh every time I think about him explaining to his wife how he spilled an entire glass of wine all over his shirt. Especially since he doesn't drink red wine."

Sam laughed, but she added, "Are you sure you're all right?"

"It wasn't that serious. I'm fine. Just pissed."

"I've got to go." She pulled some money out of her purse and gave it to Bianca. "We'll do this again soon."

"Good luck. I bet you need it."

I bet she's right.

SHE FOUND DYLAN grooming Trouble with Shadow sitting beside them. When the dog saw her he ran to her, reared up and planted his paws on her chest. Sam petted him and scolded him about jumping, though it was half-hearted.

"Hey," Dylan said. "I'll be finished in a minute."

She went to Trouble's head and rubbed his nose. "How has he been today? Any residual problems from the big to-do yesterday?"

"No. He's good. Surprised me, but Shadow's been with

him and he always manages to calm him down."

Sam couldn't decide how to start so she went with what May had told her. "I talked to May earlier. They positively identified the body found in Lake Grapevine as Gary Baxter. So obviously, he can't be the arsonist. She's ruled out four of the seven remaining suspects as well."

"That's good. Isn't it? Who are the ones that are left?"

She told him, adding, "I want to look at those three pictures again."

"Good idea. Maybe he's disguised and that's why we haven't recognized him."

When Dylan was close to finishing with Trouble, Sam decided the best way to talk to him was to put it out there.

"Dylan, we need to talk."

"Okay."

"No, I mean talk. And not over a horse."

He stood and looked over the horse's back at her. "That sounds ominous. What are we talking about?"

"Put Trouble up and then we'll discuss it. I'm going up to the house."

"All right. I'll meet you there in a minute."

During the walk up to the house, Sam tried to bolster her arguments. Dylan was not going to meekly acquiesce to her moving out. She might not have known him since they were kids, but she knew that much.

She'd just have to convince him that her moving was the best thing for both of them. Easy.

Chapter Twenty-Three

DYLAN WENT UP to the house and caught Glory just as she was leaving.

"I left dinner in the fridge," she told him.

"Thanks, Glory."

"Is everything okay with you and Sam?"

"I thought it was. Until a few minutes ago. Why?"

"She didn't seem like herself when she came in. Usually, she takes time to talk a bit but today she seemed totally preoccupied. She said hello but that was it."

"I don't know, Glory. Something's on her mind. Probably something about the fire."

"Still no news, huh?"

"Nothing definite. May's narrowed down the suspect list but we still don't know who did it."

After Glory left, Dylan went looking for Sam. He found her in the bedroom. Packing.

"What are you doing?"

"This is what I needed to talk to you about. I'm moving out."

Moving out? What the fuck? "Did we have a fight I'm not aware of?"

"Of course not."

"Then why are you leaving?"

"I'm not moving out because I'm mad at you. I'm leaving because I love you."

"Oh, well thanks for clearing that up." He leaned back against his dresser and crossed his arms over his chest, waiting for her to go on.

She stopped packing and sat on the bed. "This stalker or arsonist or whatever you want to call him isn't finished with me. He didn't succeed with the fire so he's going to try again. We're lucky he hasn't done anything else yet. But he will. And that means I'm a danger to you."

She was dead serious and this was the dumbest conclusion he'd ever heard. "You've been living here for weeks now and nothing has happened. Why are you all of a sudden moving? It doesn't make sense."

"I realize it might seem that way. I should have seen it before but I wasn't thinking clearly. The fire rattled me. I should never have moved in with you. It was thoughtless of me."

"For God's sake, Sam, this is ridiculous. I'm in no more danger now than I have been all along. You're the one who's in danger."

"Yes, I am. And I don't want you caught in the crossfire. You or anyone else here at the ranch. Or anywhere else, for that matter."

"So you're quitting your job?" He knew she wasn't but maybe she'd see how crazy this idea was.

"No. But I doubt I'll put anyone in danger at the hospital. It would be hard to get to me there."

"Right. Because this guy is so rational."

She shrugged. "Rational or not he won't find it easy to get to me at the hospital."

"So you're going to move out. Isolate yourself and make it easier for him to do what he wants with you. That's a great idea, Sam."

She ignored that. "I'm moving out until May finds the arsonist. And, Dylan, we can't see each other. I want him to think we've broken up. I know it's not what you want—"

"Not what I want?" He walked over to her. "That's the understatement of the century. You're playing right into this guy's hands. Don't you see that?"

"I'm trying to protect you," she snapped.

"Thanks very much, but I don't need any goddamned protection."

"You're being unreasonable."

"Right. And you're being perfectly logical."

"Dylan, I don't want to argue with you. My mind is made up."

Yeah, he could see that. And once she made up her mind it would be hell to get her to change it. "When is this going to happen? Now?"

"No, tomorrow. I thought about just going to a hotel. The Graff is close to the hospital. But tomorrow is soon enough. Can Shadow stay here until I find a place that will let me keep him?"

"Oh, sure. It's not like you need protection or anything. Yeah, move out and be completely alone, without even the dog to protect you. That's a fantastic idea, Sam."

"Sarcasm won't change anything. All it does is piss me off."

"Oh, really? Well, here's a shock. This whole stupid idea of yours to move out and break up is pissing me off."

"I don't want to fight with you," she repeated.

"Bullshit. You knew I'd fight you on this."

"Fine. I knew you'd fight me but I thought I could make you see reason."

Obviously, getting pissed off was not helping. Determined to convince her not to leave, he drew in a deep breath. "Sam, I am seeing reason. I understand where you're coming from but it's both unnecessary and, frankly, insulting. I don't need protecting. I'm a grown man, perfectly capable of taking care of myself. Do you think I'd ever forgive myself if you left and something happened to you?"

"Don't you understand I feel the same way? I don't know what I'd do if you were hurt because of me."

He reached for her hands and pulled her up. He put his arms around her waist and said, "I think we've reached an impasse. We're in this together, Sam. That's a good thing."

Reluctantly, she slipped her arms around him. "I should leave."

"No, you should stay with me. Leaving now won't accomplish anything except to make us both unhappy." He could sense her weakening. He kissed her cheek, the corner of her mouth, then claimed her mouth. She didn't resist. Instead she leaned in to him and kissed him back.

She pulled back and looked at him, her expression troubled. "You think you can seduce me into staying."

"I'm trying like hell. Is it working?"

"Yes, damn it."

"BUT THAT'S NOT the only reason I'm staying," Sam said.

"Okay," Dylan said, pushing her top up to pull it over her head.

She went to work on his shirt buttons. "You're right. We're involved. What affects me affects you."

He yanked his shirt off over his head. Filled his hands with her breasts. Slipped his hands down to her jeans, to unbutton and unzip them. "That's right." He pushed them down over her hips and helped her step out of them.

"He knows we're together. What's to say he won't try to hurt you to get to me, whether I leave or not?"

"Very logical." He pushed her back onto the bed, shoving her suitcase off. It landed with a thump, spilling her clothes all over the floor.

She wrapped her legs around him, feeling the strength of his erection through his jeans. "But those aren't the only reasons either."

He'd undone her bra and flung it aside. His lips traveled from her neck to her breasts. Plumping them up with his hands, he nuzzled, licked and sucked first one and then the other. She raised her hips, wrapped her legs around him even tighter.

"Dylan." She tugged on his hair until he looked at her.

"Can't we talk later?"

"No. We need to talk now."

He sighed. "You have my attention."

"I'm not sure I can leave you. I could move out, but I don't want to be without you."

His expression softened. He smiled and kissed her lips. "I love you, Sam."

"I know. I love you too."

They tugged and yanked and stripped until they were both naked. He spread her legs, pausing before he entered her. Holding her gaze as he slipped inside her, very slowly. When he was fully seated, he started the rhythm, gradually moving faster and faster.

Her climax built, pushing her higher with each deep, driving thrust. She cried out as she crested and her orgasm burst, wave after wave crashing through her.

One last thrust and he said her name as he spilled deep inside her.

Eventually, he rolled off of her, pulled her into his arms and fell asleep holding her.

Please God, don't let it be a mistake to stay with him.

SAM SLEPT RESTLESSLY that night. She tossed and turned and when she did sleep she had jumbled dreams. Not that she remembered the dreams but she knew that as unsettled as she felt, they couldn't have been very good. Dylan, she noticed, was dead to the world. He'd have to be to sleep through all her gyrations.

I'm just worried because I caved and decided to stay. Maybe I'm making a mistake but it's impossible to make myself leave when Dylan doesn't want me to and more, I don't want to.

Finally, she decided to read for a while and see if that put her to sleep. She turned on her tablet and started reading her book where she'd left off. It was a romantic suspense by one of her favorite authors, but her mind kept wandering and she couldn't focus on the book.

She kept thinking about Dylan's ex-employee, Jim Monroe. That had been a weird meeting the day before. Something about it bothered her, beyond the palpable hate she'd felt coming from him. She'd seen the man at a distance but she'd never seen him up close until she literally ran into him in the stable's office.

Why was he familiar? Why did she have the feeling she'd known him before? He couldn't be one of the final three suspects she'd told May about.

Could he?

She left the reading app and pulled up the digital photos of the three remaining suspects. Carefully, she looked through them one by one. Then she put them up side by side. The only one that struck her at all was the photo of Bill Wade. This was the same man Dylan had wondered about. The man in the photo had so much hair it was hard, if not impossible, to distinguish his features. But what would he look like clean-shaven?

She thought about his story. His wife, Sandy, had finally had enough when he nearly killed her. Her husband brought her to the ER with broken ribs, a punctured lung, and two black eyes, one swollen so badly she couldn't see out of it. He'd thought he had her completely cowed but when she'd had a moment alone with Sam, she'd begged for help to get away from him.

Sam had called the police, helped Sandy get into a women's shelter and later testified against Wade. He'd gotten a year in prison, thanks to her testimony, along with the physical evidence she provided, backing up Sandy. During the year he was incarcerated, Sandy had disappeared.

He was bound to have been furious. Angry enough to try to kill Sam when he was released? You bet. Especially if he couldn't find his ex-wife. No doubt he saw Sam as the cause of all his problems.

Wade had strange, light-colored eyes, almost silver. They weren't pretty. They were chilling. Jim Monroe's eyes were brown. Muddy brown.

He could be wearing contacts. After all, he had to realize his eyes were his most distinctive feature.

She looked at the photo again. Could Jim Monroe and Bill Wade be the same man?

"Dylan." She touched his arm, leaned closer and repeated, "Dylan. Wake up."

He slept on. Sam shook him and raised her voice. "Wake up."

He came awake with a start. "What? What's wrong?" He sat up and looked around, clearly puzzled.

"Nothing. I need you to look at something."

He rubbed his eyes. "I take it this is important."

"I wouldn't have woken you up if it wasn't." She showed him the photo of Bill Wade on her tablet. "Look at him again."

"Give me a minute. I'm still half-asleep." He yawned and shook his head. Then took the tablet from her. "Okay. Like I said before, he reminds me of someone. It's hard to tell with so much hair." He frowned, studying the picture. Finally, he said, "Jim Monroe. That's it. Give him a mustache, beard and long hair and he'd look like this man. Well, except for the eyes. This dude has strange eyes."

"Contacts. Imagine Jim Monroe with silver eyes. Freaky silver eyes."

"It could be him. You said you got a weird vibe when you saw him."

"The dogs don't like him. Shadow hates him."

Dylan smiled. "That settles it. Obviously, he's guilty."

Shadow woke up and began to whine, then pace the floor, looking at Dylan and Sam anxiously.

"What's wrong, Shadow?" He went to the door, scratched and barked. "What's that sound?" Sam asked.

Dylan listened for a moment, then jumped out of bed, pulled on his jeans, grabbed a shirt, socks and boots.

"Oh, God, is that—"

"Yes, goddamn it." He pulled on the T-shirt, then sat to put on his socks. Stood and shoved his feet into his boots. "It's the fire alarm from the stables."

Chapter Twenty-Four

FIRE. SHIT! "GODDAMN it, it's him. Monroe or Wade or whatever the hell his name is."

Calm down. The sprinkler system he'd had installed just last year was state-of-the-art. It should be, as much as it had cost. There'd been a rash of barn fires last year, with many animals dying, as well as a person. So he'd gotten the money together and not only bought the new fire alarm and sprinkler system, but he'd also modified the stables to make evacuation of the horses easier.

"Of course it's him. This is far too coincidental for it not to be the same man who set fire to my house." Sam started yanking on clothes.

"You're not coming."

"Of course I am. You need all the help you can get to evacuate the animals."

"It's a trap. You're playing into his hands."

"Don't be ridiculous. If it's a trap he wants both of us. I'm not sitting up here twiddling my thumbs while the animals are in danger." She jammed her feet into her shoes and stood.

"I put in a brand-new system last year. The sprinklers should be able to handle it, at least until the fire department can get here. Connor and Al will already be at the barn since their bunkhouse is nearby. We don't need you."

Sam didn't argue; she simply opened the bedroom door even as he talked. Shadow darted out, heading for the kitchen and the back door.

Dylan managed to grab her arm before she could follow Shadow. "Damn it, Sam. At least wait until the cops or the fire department arrive."

"You know as well as I do that minutes count in a barn fire. Stop arguing with me. You won't win." She yanked her arm out of his grasp and ran to the kitchen.

He couldn't stop her short of tying her up or something equally drastic. He caught up with her as she opened the back door. Shadow took off with the two of them following.

The scene was a madhouse. There was smoke but no flames coming from the barn. They ran inside and he saw Al at the other end of the barn, busily employing a fire extinguisher. Before he could stop her, Sam dashed off. Connor was leading Hawkeye out of his stall. There was a cacophony of sound, horses whinnying, dogs barking, the men shouting. "Where's the fire?" Dylan shouted as he reached Connor's side.

"It started in Riptide's stall. I took him out first. The sprinklers mostly took care of it, but—"

Dylan didn't wait for more. He ran to Trouble's stall, but Sam was already in with him. "Damn it, Sam! Get out of there!" Trouble was unpredictable at the best of times. God only knew what he'd do in a panic.

"Go get another horse. I've got him."

Trouble was already haltered and had a lead rope attached. Shadow was with them. Dylan hesitated, torn between leaving her with the horse and wrestling the rope away from her. But struggling with Sam might make the stallion panic even more and that was the last thing he wanted to do.

He went to Sunshine's stall and found her quivering with fear. He talked to her, soothing her as best he could, haltered her and led her out. Once outside he found Connor with another horse heading down the lane leading to a pasture some distance away. Dylan gave him Sunshine as well. "If you see Sam down there, tell her to stay put." She'd be safer with the horse and the dog rather than in the barn, especially with Wade still on the loose.

Thank God the weather had been milder with spring coming. A number of the horses were pastured overnight in another field with a shelter. He ran back in the barn, checking the stalls and other areas to make sure all the horses, dogs and people were out. As he was leaving to find Sam, he almost fell over Al, lying in the dirt close to the back barn entrance. Wondering if he'd been overcome by smoke, Dylan turned him over. "Shit! Al, how bad are you hurt?"

The smoke hadn't gotten him. He'd been shot.

"Don't know. My leg... It's bad. I took the dogs...to the bunkhouse," he panted. "That son of a bitch...Jim shot me when I got back."

"Can you walk with my help?"

"Yeah."

He couldn't. Dylan yanked off his T-shirt and gave it to Al, telling him, "Keep pressure on it. I'm getting you out of here." He locked his hands beneath Al's arms and dragged him out of the barn. It had to hurt like hell but Al didn't complain. Dylan found a lead rope and tied it around the shirt in a makeshift tourniquet. "When did this happen?" Dylan asked grimly as he worked.

"Don't know. Not...long," Al said haltingly. "He asked...where Sam was. Shot me when I didn't know."

Dylan prayed Sam had listened to Connor and stayed away, but he had a cold fear that she hadn't. "I've got to find Sam," he told Al. "The fire department should be here any moment." He hoped like hell they would.

Great. Trouble's doing God knows what, Sam is God knows where and that fucking maniac is running around with a gun looking for her.

GETTING TROUBLE DOWN to the pasture hadn't been easy, and had taken much longer than she'd hoped, but between Sam and Shadow, they'd finally managed it. He was safe now. "Shadow, stay," she told the dog, thinking he'd help calm down the stallion. As she started to leave, she ran into Connor.

"Dylan said for you to stay put."

"Are there still horses in the barn?"

"I don't know."

"Then I'm going back to help." Connor shouted after her but she ignored him. As she neared the stables she sighed in relief. No obvious flames, but there was plenty of light from every indoor and outdoor fixture that was turned on.

A heavy arm wrapped around her neck and something poked her in the back. "All alone, bitch?"

The last time she'd heard that voice had been in a courtroom, threatening her. Bill Wade. How could she have forgotten about him when he was sure to have started the fire for this very reason? "Not for long, Wade," she said with a bravado she was far from feeling.

"So you finally figured it out."

"Yes, and the police know too," she lied without a blink.

"They don't have a clue."

"Are you sure about that?" He didn't answer, but he tightened his arm around her neck. "Dylan's coming."

"You think Gallagher's gonna save you?" He laughed.

"I know he is."

"Dream on, bitch. He'll do whatever I tell him to do once he knows I've got a gun on you."

Oh, God. Of course he would—rather than risk hurting her. She fought for calm and logic. "What are you going to do, Wade? Shoot me? Kill me right away? That doesn't sound like much fun. I'd think you'd want to torture me first."

"Maybe I do. By the time I'm done you'll be begging to die."

"You'd better hurry, then."

"Why?"

"The fire department and the police will be here in five minutes."

"Bullshit."

"The fire alarm is tied in to the fire department. Don't you hear the sirens?"

His grip loosened. The wail of the sirens grew louder by the moment. She heard a furious growl. Wade screamed in pain and she twisted out of his grasp and tried to wrest the gun from him. But he broke away, frantically trying to shoot the dog hanging on to the back of one leg.

Dylan ran toward them, yelling, "Run, Sam," as he reached her. But she stood frozen, watching as Dylan hurled himself at Wade. They fought for the gun even as Shadow hung on to the back of the man's thigh like a trained K9 officer. The two men continued to struggle, first one then the other gaining the upper hand.

Unable to take her eyes off of them, Sam heard the police and fire department arrive. The muted sounds of the sirens, of people shouting, the lights flashing, water streaming—all of them faded away as she watched the desperate fight.

Shadow growled as the men fought for dominance, punctuated by grunts and groans.

She picked up a rock with a vague idea of throwing it at them, but with her luck she'd hit Dylan, so she didn't. She heard a gunshot, a cry of pain and a curse. Dylan was shirtless, she didn't know why, but she saw with sickening clarity that his left arm was bleeding and knew the bullet must have hit him.

Dylan took Wade to the ground, forcing Shadow to let go. He smashed Wade's hand in the dirt and took the gun, slowly standing up. "Shadow, no," he said when the dog advanced on the downed man, growling and snapping.

Sam ran over and grabbed hold of Shadow's collar before he could sink his teeth into another body part. "Good boy. It's okay." Then she looked at Dylan, who was weaving on his feet and still bleeding and said, "Dylan, let me help you."

"I'm okay. It's nothing." But he handed her the gun and walked away to sit on the ground.

Cursing, Wade started to get up. "If you think I won't shoot you, think again. Or I could just let Shadow loose on you." The dog stayed by her side as she'd commanded but she knew it wouldn't take much for him to go for Wade's throat. Staring at the man, the dog kept up a steady, threatening growl. Wade cursed again, but stayed where he was.

Sam shouted for a paramedic and for the police, fearing that given all the noise and commotion, they might not realize where they were or that she and Dylan needed help.

Moments later, May and another policeman arrived. "Apparently, you two didn't need my help," May said, looking at the man on the ground. "I assume this is the arsonist?"

"It's Bill Wade. And yes, he's responsible for the fire at my house and the one here, and all the stalking."

"You can't prove any of that," Wade snarled.

"Don't count on it," May told him. "Bill Wade, you're under arrest for arson and attempted murder. You have the right to remain silent…"

Sam didn't listen to the rest, but she noticed the other cop took him away, Bill still cursing. She heard the cop tell him to shut up and smiled.

"He shot Al, too," Dylan said, while the paramedics worked on him. "He's at the south end of the barn."

"Is that what happened to your shirt?"

"Yeah. Al was bleeding, so I gave him my shirt and tied a rope around it to keep pressure on it."

Critically, Sam watched the paramedics, but they clearly knew what they were doing. "How bad is it?"

"Not too bad. It's a flesh wound," Pete Larsen told her.

Sam breathed a sigh of relief. She'd been almost certain that's all it was, but it was reassuring to hear it, nonetheless.

"That's what I told you. Hurts like a bitch, though," Dylan said.

"Al's already on his way to the hospital," May said. "Connor is with the horses."

"Ow—damn, that hurts," he said, watching Pete and his partner pack his wound.

"Don't complain," Sam told him. "They're trying to make sure you don't bleed out."

"From a flesh wound? I don't think so."

"Don't be macho, Dylan."

Pete laughed. "Another ambulance will be here shortly to take you to the hospital."

"Not a chance. I can't leave now. I'll go after the fire department is sure the fire is out and I've gotten the horses settled down."

Sam didn't bother to argue. Damned stubborn man wouldn't budge until he was sure everything was taken care of. Instead she asked for a phone. "What's Sean's cell phone number?" She figured if he was working he could get the other brothers out to the ranch to help.

"You don't—"

"It's not up for discussion. Don't make me go through the hospital. Give me the number. And don't sulk."

Dylan opened his mouth and shut it. "Damn, you're tough." But he gave her the number.

Chapter Twenty-Five

"HARD TO BELIEVE the fire was only two weeks ago," Sean said to Dylan.

"It could have been a lot worse," Dylan said. Thanks to God and the new sprinkler system, fire damage had been minimal. While there had been smoke damage as well, most of the damage had been due to water, both from the sprinklers and the fire hoses the fire department employed.

"It would have taken a lot longer if you, Wyatt and Jack hadn't helped. Thanks."

All three of his brothers had pitched in after the fire. They'd taken it as a given that they would, considering that the ranch was owned by all of them even if Dylan did hold the majority share.

Sean eyed him warily. "You're not going to get mushy on me, are you?"

Dylan laughed. "Hell, no. I can say thanks without getting mushy."

"Have you heard what happened with Bill Wade? Are they going to be able to lock him up for good?"

"There's plenty of evidence against him on a shitload of charges. On top of his previous felony conviction, he'll almost certainly get a long sentence." Frowning, Dylan added, "I doubt he'll get life, though, since he didn't manage to kill anyone."

"Too bad." Catching himself, Sean added, "I mean, too bad he won't get life."

Dylan grinned. "I knew what you meant. Hopefully, he'll be too ancient when he does get out to cause any more trouble."

"Enough about that piece of shit," Sean said. "How's that new stallion?"

"He's doing really well. Sam's been working with him when she can and he's decided I'm okay."

"The fire didn't flip him out?"

"Not as much as we thought it would. He seemed to forget about it pretty quickly. Shadow calms him down."

"So you're going to breed him?"

"I think so. Not a hundred percent sure, but it's looking likely."

"When's Sam moving out?"

"She's not. Why would you think she was?"

"The women said her house was nearly finished with the remodel."

"The women?"

"Yeah. Maya told Mia who told Honey."

"First I've heard of it."

"So, you don't want her to move out?"

"What kind of a stupid-ass question is that? Of course I don't want her to move out."

"You'd better tell her, then."

Well, crap. Sam knew he wanted her to stay.

Didn't she?

SAM GOT BACK to the ranch fairly late that evening. She was tired, cranky and hungry and hoped that Dylan didn't have something he wanted to do more than eat, veg out and go to bed early. Opening the kitchen door, she stopped short at what met her eyes.

The room was lit with candles. Classical music played from speakers in the ceiling. The kitchen table was set for two with what had to be Dylan's mother's good crystal and china. A huge bowl of spring flowers stood in the center of the table. Delicious smells came from the oven, making her stomach rumble. Dylan, however, was nowhere to be seen.

He came in a few minutes later. "Hi," he said, giving her a quick hello kiss. "How was your day?"

For Dylan, he was dressed up. He wore a nice, button-down, plaid dress shirt, newish blue jeans and shiny boots that had obviously just been cleaned.

"Long. Dylan, what is all this?" She gestured to the room.

He walked over to the kitchen counter and poured them

both a glass of wine. Handing her glass to her, he said, "We've both been working long hours for the last two weeks. I thought we'd have a nice dinner."

"It's lovely." And it was a bit more than just a "nice dinner."

"Sit down and I'll bring you your meal."

"You don't need to wait on me."

"Do me a favor and just sit down."

She shrugged, sat and sipped her wine. Dylan brought their food, then sat down and tapped his glass to hers.

"This is Glory's special chicken, isn't it?" she asked.

"I told her you really liked it."

"I do."

They talked, and ate a leisurely dinner, then took their wine glasses with them to the living room.

"Where's Shadow?"

"Down at the barn. I'll go get him in a little bit."

"You don't have to do that. I can—"

"Would you just stop? I said I'd go get him."

"Fine. Why are you so grumpy?" she asked.

"I'm not. Why do you argue with everything I say?"

"I—" Frustrated, she caught herself. Technically 'I don't' would be arguing. Instead she glared at him.

"I hear your house is almost finished."

"Oh. Yes. I was going to tell you." Was that why he was cranky? Because she hadn't mentioned it? "Who told you?"

"Maya told Mia, who told Honey, who told Sean, who

told me. The grapevine in action."

"I'll say. Bianca must have told Jack. Who told Maya and so on. I just heard from the contractor today."

"What does that mean for you and me?"

"I don't understand."

"You moved in with me because your house was damaged by the fire. Not because I asked you to. So, are you going to move back to your house when it's ready?"

What the hell? "Do you want me to?"

"No, but if that's what you want—"

"I don't. I want to stay here with you."

He smiled and pulled her into his arms. "Good." He kissed her, then let go and stood up. "I'll go get Shadow."

"Dylan?" He stopped at the doorway. "Is something wrong?"

"No, why?"

Because you're acting weird as shit. "I just wondered."

"Not a thing is wrong," he said cheerfully and left the room.

Sam sipped her wine. Definitely weird. She supposed he'd tell her at some point. He came back a short time later with Shadow prancing by his side.

The dog came up to her, wiggling with delight.

"Shadow, sit," Dylan told him. "Shake," he added, when Shadow sat.

"Look at you. What a good boy you are." She looked at Dylan. "You've been training him. When did you have time?"

"Here and there. He already sat pretty well."

Sam scratched his neck. "There's something on his collar."

"You'd better see what it is."

Now she knew something was going on. And she was beginning to get an idea what it was. She parted his fur and looked. Hanging from a ribbon tied to Shadow's collar was a beautiful diamond ring. A single stone, encircled by smaller diamonds, set in platinum. "Oh, Dylan," she said unsteadily. "It's gorgeous."

"It was my mother's. If you don't like it we can get you another one."

"I love it. But aren't you forgetting something?"

"No, I don't think so."

She gave him a dirty look and he laughed. He sat beside her, untied the ribbon and held the ring up between his thumb and index finger. "Will you marry me, Sam?"

"I would love to marry you, Dylan." She held out her left hand and he slipped the ring on her finger. He kissed her, then stood and scooped her up in his arms. "What are you doing?"

"Taking you to bed. What else?"

"Good idea," she said, wrapped her arms around his neck and kissed him.

THE FRIDAY NIGHT after they got engaged, Dylan and Sam had his brothers, their wives and their children, Glory and her husband, Bianca, and Clay out to the ranch for dinner. Glory made a huge pot of spaghetti, which was a good thing because Dylan had lost count of how many of them there were. There was wine and beer—and soft drinks for the kids and Mia—as well as snacks and French bread and salad. And some kind of mystery dessert Glory wouldn't disclose.

Jack, Maya, baby Will and their two older girls, Gina and Carmen, were there. Mia was obviously pregnant now and Wyatt was pretty sappy about it. Sean had been the first of his brothers to arrive and he and Honey had immediately gone down to the barn to see Trouble. Only one person wasn't there. His sister Glenna, who was still missing.

But Glenna hadn't been home for so many things. She'd come home briefly for their father's funeral several years ago, but had left early, saying she had to get back to Argentina for work. At times he wondered if she even considered them her family anymore. She kept in touch sporadically. But he hadn't heard from her since before she disappeared in Argentina after being wrongly accused of embezzling from the ranch she'd worked at for years.

"What's wrong?" Sam asked him, slipping an arm around his waist.

"Not a thing. Why?"

"You were a million miles away." She studied him briefly. "Or maybe just South America?"

"I was thinking about Glenna, yeah." He couldn't understand why Glenna hadn't contacted him. She had to realize that none of the family would believe her guilty of embezzlement. He shook off the mood and kissed Sam. "But there's not much point in that." He joined back in one of the many ongoing conversations and tried to forget about his sister. The PI would either find her or he wouldn't, and there wasn't a damn thing he could do about that.

Later, after everyone left, he and Sam went out on the back porch to look at the moon over the mountains. Leaning back against a post with Sam in his arms, he asked, "When are we getting married?"

"You want to set a date?"

He laughed. "Isn't that what engaged people usually do?"

"Are you in a big hurry?"

"Why wait? Unless you're having second thoughts."

"Of course not." She kissed him. "Are you?"

"No way."

"Are we having a big wedding?"

"Not unless you want one. I'd be fine with family and a few friends."

Snuggling against him, she said, "That sounds perfect. I'll talk to my parents and brothers about when they can come up."

"Good. We can set a date once we know."

Dylan's phone rang. "Damn, I meant to leave it inside."

"I thought it only rang this late when it was someone on

your approved list?"

"True." Damn it. He fished it out of his pocket and looked at the caller ID. *Mitch Hardeman.* For a long moment he stared at it. Hardeman never called. The PI always texted.

He answered with, "What do you have?"

"I found her."

The line went dead.

The End

Meet The Gallaghers of Montana

Sing Me Back Home
Book 1

Love Me, Cowgirl
Book 2

The Doctor's Christmas Proposal
Book 3

The Cowboy and the Doctor
Book 4

Return of the Cowgirl
Book 5

Available now at your favorite online retailer!

About the Author

Eve Gaddy is the best-selling award-winning author of more than seventeen novels. Her books have won and been nominated for awards from Romantic Times, Golden Quill, Bookseller's Best, Holt Medallion, Texas Gold, Daphne Du Maurier and more. She was nominated for a Romantic Times Career Achievement Award for Innovative Series romance as well as winning the 2008 Romantic Times Career Achievement award for Series Storyteller of the year. Eve's books have sold over a million copies worldwide and been published in many foreign countries. Eve lives in East Texas with her husband of many years.

More from Eve:

Check out her website at EveGaddy.net

Thank you for reading

The Cowboy and the Doctor

If you enjoyed this book, you can find more from all our great authors at TulePublishing.com, or from your favorite online retailer.

TULE
PUBLISHING

Made in the USA
Middletown, DE
02 January 2019